You Never Forget Your First...

Stories of First Kills

Andrew Allen
Brian Grall
Michelle Johnston
Matthew J. Kolell
Marcus Maichle
Mark Scheef
Catalino Tolejano, II
Patrick A. Waldoch

Published by Authors Rising, LLC

Published by
Authors Rising, LLC
Milwaukee, WI
www.authorsrising.com

Cover photo , layout, and interior design by A. Weisensel

ISBN-10: 0-9830746-1-5
ISBN-13: 978-0-9830746-1-8

This book is dedicated to all aspiring writers everywhere. If you want to be published, and are willing to work hard, listen to honest feedback, and help others, come see us. :)

-Authors Rising

Thanks to family and friends for their support and understanding, and my fiancée for believing in me. Thanks also to all the authors who have inspired me with their stories, writing blogs, and hard work – from Jim Butcher, to the others in this book, and all the rest at AuthorsRising.com.

-Andrew Allen

The Id of Brian Grall would like to thank the Nobel Laureates, the board of directors, the…oh, sorry; wrong dedication.

-Brian Grall

To Derick. Thank you for always believing.

-Michelle Johnston

Thank you to Sara for her love and support. Also to Andrew for putting this together and dealing with my procrastination.

-Matthew J. Kolell

For my family, for letting me be me.

-Marcus Maichle

To my friends who convinced me to just start writing and to the other authors who shared their time and experience to help see it through: Thank you.

-Mark Scheef

I'd like to thank everyone involved on this project, especially Andrew for continuing to drive us to great results and providing structure for those of us who would be lost without it. We spent hours and hours working and providing feedback to each other, something hard but terribly rewarding on the receiving end. And finally I'd especially like to thank my son CJ for allowing me to work on this project by spending time with his Mommy Thrall - my awesome wife Carrie - when he'd rather be banging on my keyboard or pressing the alluring power button while I wrote! Thank you all!

-Catalino Tolejano, II

This story is dedicated to the authors who inspired this story: David Drake, Robert A. Heinlein, and Stephen Hunter. They all wrote (better than me, but I'm learning!) stories of men and women of conscious dealing with and trying to rise above unconscionable situations.

-Patrick A. Waldoch

CONTENTS

Crossing the Line

Andrew Allen

"Are you gonna be able to handle this, Jack?"

"Sure thing, Mr. Corazon." I replied. "Don't worry about it."

"Good man... knew you were the right man for the job. I can always count on you."

"You'll be back in three days, then?" I asked.

"By the time I'm back with the new shipment, I expect everything to be ready to roll this out on the street -- and I expect the *problem* we've discussed to be behind us. We'll have plenty to keep us busy; we can't afford any more issues like this."

"I'll handle it, sir. Have a safe trip."

And with that, Corazon climbed up into the small airplane, ordering me to cross my last line of resistance to an outright life of crime.

I had to kill a man.

I walked back to the car, and opened the door. "Get out, I'm driving." Deuce climbed out and gave me a look, then went around to the other side of the Lincoln Towncar. Like everything else about my life, the car I drove -- or was driven in, these days -- had changed quite a bit when Corazon had put me in charge a few months ago.

I'd gotten everything I always wanted... and man did it suck.

* * *

Andrew Allen

Chapter 1

As I drove away from the airport, I couldn't help but wonder when my "success" had lost it's seductive luster. I'd been trying to get into a position like this for so long. I was a key player in the organization, rewarded -- and respected -- for the impact my skills could make. "Jack, you're one of the big boys now," Corazon had said to me back in the hanger, "but along with that comes big-boy problems. Sometimes threats aren't going to be enough to eliminate those problems, and we don't have time to mess around."

"Who is this Giorna guy anyway," I had asked, "and why is he such a problem? How does he know about us?"

"Just some nut-case with a loud mouth," Corazon had replied, "and apparently we need to shut it for him."

"What about the supposed 'dangerous issues' with our drug that he was talking about? If there's anything to that, it won't go away just because he does."

"You've seen the same testing I have, Jack -- heck, you oversaw it! Was there anything to indicate the product was hurting anyone?" He'd waited for an answer, but when I didn't come up with anything, he just shrugged. "It's a love-drug, how bad can it be?!"

Deuce was staring silently out the window as we drove back towards my apartment on the waterfront. I knew he'd heard what Corazon had said, and wasn't surprised if it didn't sit too well. Until this project, Deuce had mostly been doing front-line work with clients, and he did it well. But he'd always supported me, and come along when I was put in charge of this team. I could tell he hadn't quite been comfortable, though, with "pushing drugs," -- even if Corazon assured us this wasn't a dangerous product.

I had to admit, Corazon was right on that count. Whatever Giorna, our *problem*, might believe, I hadn't once seen any bad trips, much less any of the deadly side effects the guy had been warning about. This wasn't even classified as an illegal substance... though that was mostly because it was so unknown. I'd begun very limited distribution of the new drug in one of our more selective brothels... with great effect. A "mood enhancer" Corazon called it, and it was a good description. With the right setting and reinforcement, the drug let its user completely suspend disbelief for an evening, and forget it was all just a financial transaction. For a few hours, the client got to be with someone who believed they were truly in love -- or at least that's the closest description anyone had come up with. I'd seen it work for mad, passionate love, or with sweet, tender affection -- depending on the scenario it was used in. It made the desired emotion *real* -- and amplified it -- at least for a few hours. And as far as we could tell, there were no physical side effects afterward.

Sure, a certain emotional "echo" remained for a while, but who wouldn't savor the memories of True Love? That's what I'd decided to call it, when we expanded it to wider release with the organization's "companions." In one case, a client himself had asked to take it -- but I hadn't authorized it yet for anyone who wasn't an employee. Corazon was right, though, there wasn't anything we'd seen that suggested we should slow down.

This guy, Giorna, had threatened to 'go public' about the operation. While it wasn't exactly illegal, Corazon didn't want to have to deal with 'official' attention, either. I had warned Giorna -- strongly -- about the consequences of making trouble, or sticking his nose into things. His allegations weren't going to have any impact anyway, except to get himself into a very bad situation by pissing off the Organization. I wasn't sure why Corazon was taking this guy so seriously, but I'd helped Giorna understand what was in his own best interest, and that was usually enough. I was surprised the boss believed this guy to be such a threat that he had to be eliminated. I didn't see the need, unless it was meant to be a pre-emptive example to others? But, Corazon was definitely the one in charge, and I owed my current prosperity to being in my boss' good favor.

We pulled up in front of the high-rise complex, and I got out, leaving the motor running. Deuce slid over into the driver's seat.

"You gonna do this?" he asked, refusing to meet my eyes.

"I don't see what choice I have." Silence was the only reply. "Pick me up at eight tomorrow?"

"Eight." Deuce repeated, and then pulled away.

Andrew Allen

Chapter 2

"Thanks for coming" I said to Deuce. He was back in his usual spot, serving as my driver, among other things -- but after his reaction yesterday, I hadn't been certain he'd show up today. "We're heading to our warehouse down by the river, but let's hit an Alterra first."

"What's there?" He still wasn't meeting my eyes, apparently.

"Coffee." I deadpanned, and this time I at least got an irritated glance.

"What's at the warehouse?" Deuce repeated.

"Our problem is. I told him I was willing to meet. Didn't mention what for." Truth was, I'd been up half the night trying to track this guy down through the Internet and a couple trusted contacts (hence the need for coffee). No one had seemed to know where he was, but then *I'd* gotten a message from *him*, wanting to talk. The warehouse seemed like a good place for what needed to happen. We picked up the coffee, and headed that direction. As we got close, I pulled out my 1911, worked the slide to chamber a round, and then put the safety on and tucked the pistol back into my underarm holster.

"Since when you got a gun, Jack?!" I don't think Deuce had ever seen me with one before.

"I've had it -- just never carry the thing. Never thought there was much of a need."

"I hope you know what you're doin', Jack." I sipped my coffee in silence, as I looked out the window. *So do I, Deuce*, I thought. *So do I.*

***

We pulled into the mostly-empty warehouse, and after a few moments the automated door closed behind us. There were a few boxes in a stack off to one side, with two cars and a fishing boat apparently being stored for the winter. Deuce had the radio on, to cover our awkward lack of conversation. We didn't wait long before a red light by the garage door signified someone pulled up and waiting outside. Deuce stepped out of the car to go hit the button that would open up the door. The driver pulled the car inside, and parked... but waited until the door had shut all the way before getting out of his car. He looked around with short, quick movements, sized up Deuce nervously, but apparently was satisfied there wasn't a team waiting in hiding to ambush him as he approached. I had been thinking about this a lot, and what I had in mind was far more simple.

"It was good you reconsidered, and agreed to meet," stated Giorna, "you have no idea how bad this thing is." He held out his hand to shake.

I surprised him with a punch to the gut instead, then swept his suddenly unsteady legs out from under him. Giorna went down hard on the concrete, with a cry of pain. "You're the one who has no idea how bad this is," I said, and delivered a solid kick to Giorna's side as he lay curled up on the ground. I took a step back, as the other man lay groaning. "Do I have your attention now?" I yelled. "I thought I was pretty clear the other day in telling you to BACK OFF."

"You... you don't understand..." he panted, holding his side as he struggled to talk, "your 'True Love' is .... is killing people!"

"Impossible!" I spat the word down at him. I had to make this convincing, make Giorna believe I'd kill him, or the man would never back down. "Get him up."

Deuce might have his misgivings, but he'd never failed to back me in action. He grabbed Giorna's jacket, and hauled him to his unsteady feet.

"I know every user," I continued through clenched teeth, "and they're all" (right jab to the midsection) "...just" (followed by a left) "... fine!" I punctuated this last word with another hit to Giorna's stomach. The man tried to go down again, but Deuce held him up. Giorna settled for throwing up instead.

"Oh, god, please..." he held up a hand, the other arm clutching his stomach, "stop... you've got to listen to me... those gangers on the news the other night. The massacre... that was no normal fight. They were on True Love." He seemed to be getting a hold of himself. Not good. "Trust me, I know this drug. You can't put it out on the street."

This was just crazy. I'd carefully controlled every single dose of the drug Corazon had given me, and there was no way any of it made its way to the street. I needed to get my point across to this lunatic once and for all. I grabbed Giorna's lapels, and without letting go, kneed him squarely in the groin. "Shut up and *you* listen! Whatever you might think, you don't know this drug – there's never been anything like it before. After my boss gets back tomorrow, it's going to be on the streets, and there's nothing you can do about it. If you're not outta town by then, you're a dead man." I moved in close to his face. "Do you believe me?" The man looked up at me, looked in my eyes, and nodded. One more solid hit should do it. I went for his face this time. As expected, Giorna went down, out cold.

Chapter 3

I shook out my hand, "Christ! That hurt..." and looked at Deuce, who had bent down to check on the man on the concrete. "Next time I'm going to try that 'hit him with the gun' thing. Let's get out of here."

"We're leaving?" in his surprise, Deuce forgot to avoid looking at me for a moment.

"Yeah. He should be fine, none of that was too serious. Roll him on his side, and when he wakes up, he'll be gone before the night's through." I examined my hand a bit more closely. "I'm gonna need to stop and get ice for this."

***

Another silent car ride, this time we left the radio off. Deuce had stopped at a fast food place, but just sat in the car. I had to go in and order a large soda, then dump it by the car, and put my hand in the cup of ice. As we headed back to my place, I barely noticed the lack of conversation... I was lost in my own thoughts anyway.

Problem was, I *had* heard about the gang thing Giorna mentioned. Two local groups that had occasional scuffles in the past, maybe someone had even gotten killed once or twice -- but nothing like what had happened this time. One group had encountered the other, who knows how or why, but the situation had apparently quickly escalated beyond all control. The first group had gone completely berserk, and wiped out the others. And the amount of damage was staggering, to both sides. These guys had gone at it with absolutely everything they had, and no one had the slightest idea why. One of the survivors vehemently told the cops 'it was worth it' …. though when pressed later he couldn't seem to come up with any good reason why.

Could this really have had something to do with True Love? Had rivals gotten jealous over a companion that both thought was in love with them? I still didn't see how the drug could have been the cause... and unless it had been stolen before Corazon had released the test batch to me, I was sure none of the supply was missing. I couldn't believe any of the test users would have smuggled out doses of the drug – I'd picked them because they were loyal to me. Besides not wanting to risk defying Corazon, my few testers knew how much I had riding on this. Corazon had put me in charge, but this was still my first big project. I was still proving myself to him. My test users wouldn't do that to me.

With this afternoon's episode, however, I'd risked much more potential harm to my reputation than anyone else could cause. If Corazon found out I hadn't killed Giorna, he'd treat it like I'd committed outright mutiny. Maybe *I* should be the one leaving town before tomorrow... eh, I'd better look into the possibility of any missing True Love, and figure out if there was more to the events I'd helped put in motion than I realized.

We pulled up again to the apartment, and just sat for a moment.

"When did we slip over the edge and become thugs?" Deuce asked rhetorically.

"Hey," I got out of the car, then turned back, "I didn't kill him."

Chapter 4

Deuce pulled up again late the next afternoon. He grunted noncommittally as I got into the car.

"We've got about an hour before Corazon's plane is due in," I said, "so there should be plenty of time to get to the hangar." Deuce turned the car around and began driving towards the airport. I remembered just a few days ago, our easy, joking discussions. Now there was a barrier, a wall between the two of us. I felt like Deuce had been taking longer to do things over the last two days... for the first time thinking about whether or not to do as I asked him. It was probably only a matter of time before he decided not to. His best bet would be to just leave, without saying anything. I'd be sad to see him go, but he'd get far before anyone else really noticed and considered going after him.

With the silence of the car, my mind went again to the question I'd been wrestling with. How did Giorna, this random guy, know so much about True Love, when I had never had anything to do with him? I knew personally, and had hand-picked, the few people involved. From the moment Corazon passed the drug to me, I knew where it had been. Giorna must have been at one of the houses... where else could he come into contact with it? Had he stolen some, and somehow used it? Was there any reason to believe it really was behind the gang incident? Would there be more of them? I didn't know, but had decided I needed to bring it up to Corazon, and see what he said about it.

I turned that over in my head all the way to the airport. As we parked inside the hangar, I still hadn't come up with an easy way to do it.

"Bathroom" said Deuce, getting out. Would he be coming back? I checked the time on my phone. The plane should be arriving any minute. It was getting dark quickly, so I decided I'd go turn on the hangar lights. Just after I did, a shot rang out. I spun, dropped into a crouch, and looked for the source of the threat. Was it Deuce?

"Don't move," called a voice, "lie down." What?! "I won't miss next time." I held up my hands as I looked toward the source of the voice. I couldn't believe it. Limping towards me was... Giorna!?

"You idiot!" I almost shouted, "I let you go, why the hell would you come back?!"

"You have to make a stand sometime." he replied, "When you said Corazon was coming back, and the product would hit the streets, I put two and two together."

"But what do you think you can do?" My heart was pounding, but I tried to seem in control of the situation.

"As soon as he's here, I can kill the two of you. Or, I suppose, I could just get you out of the way right now."

Thankfully, Deuce chose that moment to club Giorna over the head. He must have heard the shot on his way back from the bathroom, and he crept up while Giorna was focused on me.

"Thanks, Deuce." The adrenaline was still going strong as I walked over and picked up Giorna's gun. "I owe you." I tucked it into my waistband at the small of my back, then looked down at Giorna's half-conscious form. "Unbelievable. We'd better get him out of here before Corazon shows up."

"Too late." said Deuce, and pointed to where the small jet could already be seen taxiing in our direction.

"Dammit!" I swore, "I guess I'd better go meet him."

Chapter 5

The small plane taxied to a stop, its lights bright even on the well-lit tarmac. Apart from two standard-looking delivery vans waiting near where the plane had come to rest, the area was surprisingly deserted. Flights at this hour were unusual at the small airport, but I thought there ought to be more people around anyway. Maybe Corazon had bought off the normal crew, to make it easier to unload the shipment. The single door unfolded, and Owens – one of Corazon's bodyguards – came out first. He nodded to me, and stepped to the side. This was it... this was when I'd have to make my stand, before the product was distributed, before it hit the streets. A familiar figure appeared in the doorway, and I steeled myself for what was about to come.

"Welcome back, Mr. Corazon. How was your trip?"

"Productive, Jack. As expected." His other bodyguard came down behind him. "Did everything go alright here?"

I hesitated for a moment, "For the most part, sir."

Corazon gave me a hard look, then turned to the pair that had come out of the plane with him. "We've got to be out of here quickly, why don't you two have the pilot help you get the shipment loaded in the vans, while Jack and I step inside and catch up." Owens nodded, and Corazon turned and began walking toward the hangar. I quickly followed. "What about our ... *situation*, Jack?" He asked it over his shoulder, without turning to look back at me. There was an edge to his voice now, not quite as pleasant as a moment before. I hurried to follow. This wasn't how I'd wanted this discussion to go.

"Don't worry sir," I responded, as we reached the hanger door, "we've got him. He claims--"

"YOU'VE 'GOT' HIM?!" Now he whirled back around, eyes blazing. "That was NOT how this was supposed to be 'handled,' Jack. Where is he?"

"Being held inside. He said he has proof the product has been being tested outside the Houses? Do you know what he's talking about?"

"Give me your gun, Jack." Uh oh, I thought, I might have gone too far, too fast...

"I'd hate to think someone is stealing this out from under us."

"Your gun." He held out his hand.

"Yes, Sir." I handed it over. We walked inside the hanger, and there off to the side were Deuce and Giorna. The latter was sitting against the wall, still looking groggy as he recovered from the take-down. Deuce stood watch a few yards away.

As we approached, Giorna's eyes widened, as he saw Corazon walking up with the gun. He stopped far enough away to be well out of reach.

"I'm very disappointed, Jack. I thought I could count on you." Corazon turned to face me. "Why is he still alive?"

"Sir, I thought his information might be important," my automatic tendency to smooth-talk my way through kicked in. "If he really knows about our supply getting out through back-door channels this early in our plan, I thought you'd better hear it."

Corazon looked skeptical. "That's a pretty weak story for why you didn't follow through. You getting cold feet on me, or just don't want to get your hands dirty?" Deuce and Giorna watched this exchange in silence, and the area seemed to become very still.

"You're not concerned about the source of the extra product?..." I finally, slowly connected the dots "because... it had to

18

come from you." Suddenly it all made sense. "You've got someone slipping this to gangers, and inciting rage, instead of the lust we're creating in the houses." Corazon didn't deny it. "Didn't you hear about the massacre a few nights ago? Sir, if that's true, we can't let this get into circulation outside the houses. We've got to change plans before this gets out of hand. Think of what could happen."

"I do think of it, Jack." Corazon was watching me carefully. "This is the ultimate manipulation drug. We can make anyone feel anything we want. Rage. Lust. Gratitude. Fear ... I think of what will happen... of how much money we'll make off this. The people who want that power are going to pay a lot for it."

"No, you can't!" Giorna finally spoke up, and struggled shakily to his feet. "That's not what I designed it for. We can't trust anyone with that! What if I had slipped it into *your* drink... right before someone told you there was only one way out of your agonizing depression, and pointed you at a cliff?"

"He's right." I said, finally making a firmer stand, "we can't do this."

"No, he's not right" replied Corazon with clipped words, his eyes narrowed. Then he shot Giorna in the head. "He's dead."

Corazon closed his eyes for a moment, and let out a slow breath. "I feel better already... someday maybe you should try that, Jack." He pulled out a handkerchief, and handed it – and my gun -- to Deuce. "Here, clean that... we *are* doing it, Jack, and there's nothing you can do about it." He glanced at Giorna's body, "I should have done that as soon as he'd finished making the first batch." He looked back up at me. "You'd better realize you've got no choice, and get on board -- or I'll replace you with the next person in line. And then keep going anyway." He pulled out his cell phone. "I'll get Owens to clean this up." He glanced at me, "yes, Jack, he does *that*, too."

As my boss began to punch numbers into the phone, I pulled out the gun I'd confiscated from Giorna, and shot Corazon dead center.

He hit the concrete with a look of disbelief still on his face. I picked up Corazon's phone, and walked over to place the gun in Giorna's hand, feeling a lot calmer all of a sudden. I looked back at my boss' body, and realized he was right. I did feel better.

"Hello, Mr. Corazon?" said the voice on the other end, as the phone connected.

"Owens, this is Cassanova. Something just happened..." I projected cold, commanding anger... it was important to get this right, "that lunatic showed up at the hangar, gunning for us. I put a bullet in his head, but Corazon is dead. I'm in charge of this operation now, and I need you in here right away to get this taken care of."

I met Deuce's eyes, and this time the other man didn't look away. There was no mistaking I'd crossed a line, but I didn't know if Deuce was still with me on this side of it. After a moment, he nodded, and handed me back my gun.

Maybe I could still make a difference after all.

*A student of martial arts, and a multi-sport enthusiast, **Andrew Allen** has realized that you don't have to be good at your hobbies to enjoy them immensely. He has two incredible daughters who love to read, and the greatest fiancée in the world.*

Acheron: The Stream of Woe

Brian Grall

PROLOGUE
All Traveled Roads Lead Underground

It is about ten o'clock on a cold, damp mid-spring night in Milwaukee, WI. The sky is clear, sporting a good number of stars and the night air is light with the fragrance of summer approaching after a long, mind-numbingly cold winter. The remnants of winter still surround all the homes and buildings of the city, fighting the coming warmth to the bitter end.

A man in his mid 20's is returning home from a night's work at the local U-Sav Drug store, where he is an assistant manager. His name is Dave Van Hoffman and he is very tired, coming off a long twelve hour day, where the other assistant manager who was supposed to relieve him, called in sick. He also has a date coming in the next fifteen minutes and desperately needs a shower to wash the work day off him.

Like any typical night, he pulls into his apartment complex's parking lot. He parks his black Chrysler Sebring into its usual stall, exits the car and begins to walk to his mailbox. As he's moving towards the outdoor community mailbox, he hears the familiar noises of the clanking of his car keys, his own footsteps and two other car doors closing. He then hears some guys speaking, not knowing exactly where this is coming from, he turns around to check it out, sees two men approaching the mailbox from across the lot, one much huskier than the other and then turns back towards his box to finish retrieving his mail. This is a shared lot so he thinks nothing of the approaching men, only of the shower and date to follow.

This ends up not being his typical night.

"HEY!" One of the men says in a nervously deep voice. Dave

turns around again to see the bigger of the two men pointing a gun sideways at him, telling him to get on the ground, face first. Continuing, Number One tells him to "give us the money."

Thinking he has him mixed up with someone else Dave says "I don't owe you any money". Number One replies "That's not what I'm talking about."

Without saying a word, Number Two walks behind Dave and grabs his arms behind his back, handcuffs him, then they both walk him to their car with the gun pressed behind his left ear and proceed to stuff him in a trunk, with no explanations as to why. As the trunk closes on Dave, he sees his date's car pulling into the lot.

Dave's head is on the driver's side of the car and loud Rap music is blasting in his left ear. As they're leaving his apartment complex, Dave is able to stay with the driver's directions for what he perceives as a few blocks and then loses his way almost as quickly. He was recalling some old cop-drama's he's seen on TV, hoping he would be the surviving victim and is able to give the police some directions as to where they went.

It's almost entirely dark inside except for a slight crack of light from the trunk lid and soft red glow of the taillights. The road they are on is potholed and he can hear other traffic around him. Dave begins to push his feet up against the roof of the trunk. He sees a little more light, but then thinks "what happens if I get it open and jump out? Will I get hit by a car behind me? Will I get shot if I try to run away and they chase me?" Dave ends up just staying inside, praying to God to help him get out of it. The only other thing he can think of is, "If I keep my cool, will they?"

At that moment, the car turns off the paved road and onto what feels like a dirt road, due to the many bumps he's feeling in the trunk. The car suddenly stops, doors open and he feels bodies get out of the car and Dave thinks; "this is it…I'm going to be killed in some random hate crime and I'll be left to rot in the middle of nowhere".

Seconds later, as if the thugs could read his mind, the men get back in the car and continue; like a Chinese fire drill.

A few more minutes pass (which seem an eternity, where he promises God he'll do whatever He wants if He'll get him out of this alive). The car stops again, the thugs get out and open the trunk. All he sees are parking lot lights in the foreground and elevated lights further in the background and instantly knows he's at Lincoln Park. A park where he's played baseball on and knows he's only about five minutes from his store. The thugs are standing to the rear driver's side in front of the parking lot light where Dave's head is and finally tell him their plans.

"We want the money in the bottom of the safe," Number One says.

Dave replies quickly, but calmly, "I can't get that open without the key that the armored truck guys have. If you want to take it from them, be my guest." He says with a little promise in his voice.

"How much you got on top?" asks Number One, noticing that Number Two doesn't offer much to the situation.

"About a thousand including rolled coins. Look, I can get you in the store and you can take what you want." They close the trunk, get back into the car and crank that god-awful music again. Dave hears the two of them arguing over the music, and then they turn the music off and reopen the trunk.

"We're gonna do that" says Number One and closes the trunk yet again.

The next time it opens, he notices he's in the dimly lit alley behind the U-Sav Drug store, and they forcibly pull him out of the trunk. Dave quickly looks around and sees that there's nobody in sight to yell for help, save for the shadow in the neighboring yard that could either be a man or a tree. Dave decides to play it safe and keeps quiet.

Number One still has the gun and goes into the store with Dave, leaving Number Two shrinking into the shadows of the store with the car.

Dave digs his keys out of his pocket and unlocks the sliding glass doors. He then disarms the alarm and is led to the safe, with Number One walking closely behind. They walk past all the new springtime patio chairs and houseplants that Dave just set up earlier that day. Dave pushes open the small hinged door that separates the register area from the store patrons and takes two more steps to the front of the safe.

"You sure you can't get us in the bottom of the safe man?" Questions Number One in a disbelieving tone. Dave replies in a calm but direct voice, "No matter what you do to me, I can't get you in there without that armored truck key".

Dave gets the safe door open then is pulled out of the way by Number One slamming him into the register, who then proceeds to empty the upper half with the vigor of a sweepstakes contestant into a shopping bag. He tosses the money inside then grabs another bag to support it so it won't break open.

Number One finishes his shopping spree, grabs a couple packs of Newport's saying with a sneer, "these are for me, screw my friend and now with my first kill, I'm a Death Broker" then shoots Dave in the face, blowing his nose clear through the back of his skull, killing him before he hits the floor.

CANTO I
Pilot of the Livid Marsh

SLOSH.…...……....…...SLOSH.............................SLOSH.…...………....

A distinct repeating sound breaks through the heavy, hushed unbending fog. The light-gray fog is thick, so thick that one is unable to observe distances. It is tremendously damp and feverishly cool; seeming to spray light beads of water on everything it touches. There is only an illusion of sky. Nor is there any discernable landscape features or animal noises coming from a space housing an artery of water that should have at least some of these sounds. A charcoal tinted object comes into view, gradually piercing the haze.

SLOSH.…...……....…...SLOSH.............................SLOSH.…...………....

As the object nears, one can make out the image of a man standing in a boat, pushing it along the silky surface of the water with his staff. The surface of the water is smooth as glass and the staff or the boat doesn't make any ripples as it skims across; leading one to believe that they would not need to use a boat at all.

SLOSH.…...……....…...SLOSH.............................SLOSH.…...………....

A boat the size of a small car approaches. The front is the largest part of the boat and is five feet tall, with an exposed spine on the rounded nose that upturns like a squared off scythe. The wood is observably old with many small holes perforating the hull and may give way to the stresses of the water at any moment, but somehow remains intact. The rest of the boat narrows towards the back where the boatman stands.

SLOSH.......*SLOSH*.......*SLOSH*.......is the sound the staff makes through the putrid, murky, silver-gray water known as Acheron, the river of woe.

The smooth, worn down staff is held in the hands of a being that, although appears human, that is the thing that he is farthest from. Its hands are wrapped in soiled, wet linen, trying to cover up but exposing the decaying flesh and bone beneath. The hands move as if in unrelenting pain, pushing the staff into the water, culminating in the stagnant *SLOSH* sound.

The arms the hands are attached to are riddled with sores and pustules, draped by a cloak that can best be described as resembling afterbirth with the color of its skin being grayish-purple and smells of rotting meat.

SLOSH.....…….....…....*SLOSH*.............................*SLOSH*.....………....

The body of the boatman has large shoulders and is hunched over from the monotonous comings and goings of the boat he steers in the still, silver-gray water.

SLOSH.....…….....…....*SLOSH*.............................*SLOSH*.....………....

As the boat comes ever closer, a being looks at its feet and realizes that they're standing on the shore, watching as the boat closes the gap. The being notices that the cloak covering the body also has a hood draped over the head of the boatman. This hood conceals the boatman's facial features so well that it appears to not allow light to shine upon its face at all; no matter which direction it turns its head. All that can be seen is a pair of eyes ringed about with wheels of flame.

SLOSH.....………....*SLOSH*.............................*skreeeeeek, THOOM*.

The boat comes screeching to a halt on the gravel shore, where it has stopped every time there are passengers prepared to board. The boatman straightens up to address the passengers and speaks in a voice extraordinarily uninviting.

"Abandon all hope, ye who enter here".

Brian Grall

CANTO II
The Caretaker of Souls

The boatman stares at his would be fare for what seems like centuries. One brave soul hesitatingly begs the question, "Who are you?"

"I am Charon; the last servant of the gods" the shrouded figure tells the spectators gathered on the shore. "You 'shades' are here because someone has paid for your interment on Earth. I am here to ferry you to the plains of Elysium, where you will be paying for your former lives above ground".

Upon hearing this, some displeased murmuring begins among the shades. Charon bows his head and says, "Woe to you, corrupted souls! Forget your hope of ever seeing Heaven; I come to lead you to the other shore, to the eternal dark, to fire and frost". These exhausted spirits had lost their color and gnashed their teeth upon hearing Charon's cruel words.

One shade, which stands a few shades apart from Charon, interrupts and says, "Are we dead?" Charon responds by staring blankly.

The same quivering shade asks "For how long?"

"For time without end!" booms the boatman in an even more revolted tone. "All who stand before these doors have been judged and will proceed to their illumination; wherever that may lie".

"Am I in Hell?" asks a surprisingly composed shade.

The boatman then raises his head glaring his primordial eyes at that shade and grinning with his decrepit lips declares "Not yet".

CANTO III
Restless In Peace

"ROAAAAAAAAAAAAAAAAAAAAAAAAHHHHHHHHH HHRRRRRRR"

The shades hear a stadium's worth of commotion coming from their right and left and upon looking around in fear and bewilderment, focus on thousands upon thousands more shades moving toward them at great speed. These are lost souls who haven't been buried properly on earth, for a variety of reasons; no family or friends, destitute, missing or just died and left where they fell. They have not been rewarded and their bodies are still rotting away; as are their souls.

Charon steps out of his vessel, shoving his way through the shades waiting along the riverbank, raises his poled right hand above him and bellows, "Back you forsaken souls!"

The charge of the deserted continues to close in on the group. The shades begin to panic, clamoring over one another and charging the boat to get away from the stampede. This was not unexpected by the hooded figure, who's been doing this task since time immemorial, who just let them pass by.

Charon turns back on the frenzied crowd and speaks. "Make thee way to the land of life and haunt your masters, then return for your prize".

Ancient legends tell of the souls that are allowed to step onto Charon's boat, need pay him with an obol or coin that was placed into the mouth or onto the eyes of the deceased. That coin was then given to Charon by that soul in order to proceed to their eternal rest. If the soul hasn't had a proper burial, then it'd have to find a way to get back to Earth and locate the appropriate person to attend them. If unable to track down said person, the soul would come back and stay upon the shoreline for one hundred years, upon only then would the soul be allowed into the ferry and onto the Netherworld.

As Charon finished, the souls were cut off by Cerberus, the giant three-headed guard dog of the Netherworld, who plucked a soul that was closest to the riverbank and furthest away from him, just to demonstrate his reach. He promptly tore that soul in half, devouring it in plain sight of the rest of the mob. This beast was unique and a gift from Hades, the god of the Underworld, to prevent the disobedience of the damned while guarding the gateway from the land of the living.

Upon viewing this grisly banquet, most of the shades stopped immediately with a foolish few remaining to approach Charon, who with the speed, strength and accuracy of an Olympic javelin athlete, simply skewered the three with his pole; jamming them and the pole into the grimy dirt where the top soul pressed onto the one beneath, then the one beneath that onto the clay, where they would remain together as a totem for the centuries to come, being tortured both physically and mentally by Cerberus and Charon as well as the unremitting line of passengers.

Cerberus knew his job and performed it with precision, for if a soul kept pressing the ferryman, he'd take a giant paw and crush the soul in the slimy dirt. Then he'd get playful with it and decide to violently shake it like a newly caught squirrel in one of its eager mouths, tear the stuffing out the body to see what it was made of and roll over it, devouring the soul's entrails in the process. Cerberus would then pick the pieces of the soul up and bring it back to the entrance to the Underworld where he made his home, gnawing on them like a treat that never loses its flavor. The souls would then be his until he was bored playing with it, wherein the soul was able to leave, provided there was anything left to aid its movement. Either way, the soul still had to make it to the shoreline, just to discover its fate.

As Cerberus drools over this soul while eyeing some other tasty morsels, Charon waves a plague-ridden arm and instructs the three shades to enter his boat.

As the first shade stumbles into the boat, it notices there are five benches spanning the width of it, where there's more room on the front benches tapering off to the rear, but there is room for only one next to the boatman. The shade begins to wonder why this is, but has not the courage to ask. This is also the shade Charon orders to take that lonely last seat.

Once the shade takes its seat next to the boatman's perch, it begins to realize that from this angle, the boat is eerily reminiscent of a coffin. That makes this shade even more uneasy than it was before, wishing it was anyplace other than this.

Seeing the unending dread in the first shade's eyes, the remaining two reluctantly enter the vessel and take their seats as directed in rows one and three.

Before climbing aboard the boat, Charon approaches the three blighted shades that are stuck to the dirt like a pin in a pegboard. Reaching for his soul-piercing kebab and terrifying the shades attached to it even further, Charon breaks off a piece, mixes it with the dirt and fusty water and stretches it out into another staff to propel his craft and cargo.

Incredulously, the boatman then steps onto the water's surface moving towards the rear of the ferry, steps over the edge and takes his place next to the petrified shade on row five. With a mighty heave from the shoreline, he begins their final voyage.

The first stop for the crew of the damned is a quick one. The first shade off is last on the boat. This soul's funeral happened much too early in their young life and is able to recall the events that happened, though not horrifying but heartbreaking.

Upon glancing back at the shoreline, the shades still see the shouting swarm of shades gathered near the waters edge, but still keeping a safe distance from Cerberus.

Charon steers the death-boat towards the adjacent shore bordering the Acheron which is where this first shade disembarks. As it steps foot onto the shoreline, the shade materializes into the form of a beautiful but sad young woman, holding her stomach as she turns towards the vessel with tears streaming down her youthful face, as a torrent of emotions overwhelm her.

Charon speaks to the young woman in a nature directly opposite his character. "Go now girl and weep no more, for you no longer need to pay for your soul, you did nothing wrong. Thanks to your desire to save your child, your daughter is alive and well with her father growing by the day; though missing you terribly. You will be reunited once again". And with that, the boat pushes onward passing through the River Cocytus and onto their next destination, the River Phlegethon.

CANTO IV
No Good Soul Ever Takes Its Passage Here

Journeying on, the remaining two shades find that the mist is dreadfully thick all around the boat and get few glimpses of the landscape it travels through. Though what little the shades can see is utterly foreboding, one can make out steep, sharp rocks that have combined to form an inverse sheer cliff, which could be hundreds or thousands of feet up from the waters edge.

dum…………………..dum………………..dum….
……..dum…...dum…..dum…dum..

The temperature in this region increases drastically where there is heat and steam everywhere. Even the decaying boat seems to be drying out, destined to become a large piece of driftwood.

AaaahhhhhhhhhhhhhhhhhhhhhhhhhhhhhhhhhhhhhhhhhhhhhHHHHH
HHHHHHHHHHHHHHHHHHHhhhhhhhhhhhhhhhhhhhhhhhhhHHHHHHH
HHHHHHHHHHHHHHHHHHhhhhhhh……
dum..dum…dum..dum….dum..dum….dum…
dum..dum..dum..dum..dum..dum..dum..dum

AaaahhhhhhhhhhhhhhhhhhhhhhhhhhhhhhhhhhhhhhhhhhhhhHHHHH
HHHHHHHHHHHHHHHHHHHhhhhhhhhhhhhhhhhhhhhhhhhhHHHHHHH
*HHHHHHHHHHHHHHHHHHhhhhhhh……*What was once deathly silent has begun to be filled with a multitude of thunderous whispers. The ferried souls begin to look around as if trying to find the source of these sounds but cannot. The sounds are coming from all angles, bouncing off the ancient stone walls and redirecting above the surface of the water. All they can do is hold their shadowy heads in hushed agony as the whispering increases.

*AaaahhhhhhhhhhhhhhhhhhhhhhhhhhhhhhhhhhhhhhhhhhhhHHHHHHHH
HHHHHHHHHHHHHHHHhhhhhhhhhhhhhhhhhhhhhhhhHHHHHHHH
HHHHHHHHHHHHHHhhhhhhh…*

dum..dum..dum..dum..dum..dum..dum..dum..dum..dum..dum..dum.
.dum..dum..dum..dum

As the shades become adjusted and the noises begin to level off,
they're able to focus on the source of the racket. The base sounds
continue as the boat bobs back and forth, as if being struck in the
water by thick tree branches. Glancing down, they see heads floating
in the reddish water, one on top of the other like a gravel road, with an
occasional mouth bubbling past the surface where one of billions of
the groans originates. They both recoil in terror.

Looking up, around and outward, the souls become aware that the
entire river is littered with bobbing heads dancing to a tune of moans
in a river of boiling blood.

"This is the River Phlegathon. Here are murderers and tyrants:
people who through their violent deeds in life caused hot blood to flow
and now themselves are sunk in a river of blood that boils souls", says
Charon grimly to the horrified travelers. A particular whisper begins
to increase. "The most vile and wicked human beings inhabit this
cesspool. Alexander the Great, Gengis Khan, Elizabeth Bathory, John
Wilkes Booth, Adolf Hitler, Jeffery Dahmer, Saddam Hussein,
Pharoahs, Kings and Queens, Czars, assassins and millions of other
malevolent citizens all reside here", he continues.

As soon as the ferryman finishes his statement, one whisper gains
strength, breaks through the hoarse commotion and repeats and repeats
- *"These are for me, screw my friend and now with my first kill, I'm a
Death Broker - these are for me, screw my friend and now with my
first kill, I'm a Death Broker - these are for me, screw my friend and
now with my first kill, I'm a Death Broker"*. Hearing this, one shade
becomes agitated and the other is puzzled.

With this, Charon looks down at the shade sitting next to him in the fifth row and growls, "Get out of my vessel!"

The shade sits petrified looking at the slushy red water and says fearfully, "What did I do? I don't belong here! Where should I go?"

The boatman furiously retorts "In the rancid stew, where evil belongs!" And faster than the shade can see, cracks his staff across the nose of the shade, knocking it overboard into the abysmal river.

Immediately upon slapping the crimson soup, the shade solidifies and sinks to join its brethren. Soon, some bubbles begin to leech to the surface, belch and a head breaks the red syrupy plane, followed by eyes, a nose and a wrecked, revolting howl coming from the mouth of Number One's soul.

"He shall rot here for perpetuity and his spirit shall never be rewarded" Charon says as he pushes off to his final delivery.

AaaahhhhhhhhhhhhhhhhhhhhhhhhhhhhhhhhhhhhhhhhhhhHHHHH HHHHHHHHHHHHHHHHHHHhhhhhhhhhhhhhhhhhhhhhhhhHHHHHH HHHHHHHHHHHHHHHHhhhhhhh...

dum..dum..dum...dum...dum....dum....dum.....dum......
dum.......dum........dum

The number of heads bumping against the hull decreases and the moans increase yet again as they leave this stink behind.

Brian Grall

CANTO V
And As Life Is To The Living, So Death Is To The Dead

*AaaahhhhhhhhhhhhhhhhhhhhhhhhhhhhhhhhhhhhhhhhhhhHHHHHHHH
HHHHHHHHHHHHHHHHhhhhhhhhhhhhhhhhhhhhhhhhHHHHHHHH
HHHHHHHHHHHHHHhhhhhhh......*
dum…..dum……dum…….dum……..………...dum..
……………..dum………….……..

At last there is one shade remaining.

*Aaaahhhhhhhhhhhhhhhhhhhhhhhhhhhhhhhhhhhhhhhhhhhhhhhhhhh
hhhhhhhh*
dum………………………dum……………………………
……………………
Aaaahhhhhhhhhhhhhhhhhhhhhhhhhhhhhhhhhhhhhhhhhh…………………
………*

The noises taper off and the steam and heat relinquishes its grasp as the ferry leaves the River Phlegethon.

The shade talks hopelessly to its shapeless hands but loud enough for Charon to hear. "I can't take any more of this. I don't know who I am and what I did to end up here".

Charon speaks calmly, running a cold chill down the darkened back of the shade. "Fear not, son of man. Your journey is coming to an end and it will not be as the same as the previous traveler".

"How do you know these things?" asks the final shade.

"I know what the gods know about every soul above, below and yet to be. I have seen their character and will be there when they need me; for that is my duty". Charon replies to the depressed soul as they cross the threshold of the River Lethe.

The boat is passing through extraordinarily calm waters now, seeming as if it's going no place fast. The sheer rock cliffs have shrunk from the ceiling and seem to be less daunting with more sweeping and rolling hills with sod hanging over the edges. The manner of this province feels light and blissful. The sky also seems to be opening as a passing storm reveals the brighter day.

murrrrrrrrrrr………..murrrrrr………...murrrrrrrrrrrr………..murrrrrrrrrrr……..

Ahead of the boat and around the bend in the river, a rounded and surprisingly welcoming cave comes into view. This prompts the shade to turn back at Charon and ask "are we going through there?" Where Charon only nods his head in agreement.

murrrrrrrrrrrr………..murrrrrr………...murrrrrrrrrrrr………..murrrrrrrrrrr……..a soft slight murmuring is heard coming from the cavern ahead.

"This is the River Lethe that borders the plains of Elysium, the final resting place of the virtuous. At the forefront is the cave of Hypnos the god of sleep, where you will drink of its waters allowing the memories of your earthly life to be released and then your soul will begin its reincarnation" the boatman explains. "Upon drinking the water, you will be able to relive all the moments of your life and death as it was, one final time before your soul's transformation. It may seem like an eternity, but I assure you, it shall be virtually instantaneous" Charon continues.

murrrrrrrrrrrr………..murrrrrr………...murrrrrrrrrrrr………..murrrrrrrrrrr……..murrrrrrrrrrrr…
……..murrrrrr………..

Even though they are closing in on the mouth of the cave, the murmuring continues but curiously doesn't increase in volume, just remains that soft and steady hum.

murrrrrrrrrrrr..........murrrrrr...........murrrrrrrrrrrr..........murrrrrrrrrrr........
murrrrrrrrrrrr..........murrrrrr...........

As the boat nears closer to the Elysium shoreline, the final shade is able to see other souls that appear to be walking around blissfully ignorant to the journey taking them here. They all seem as if they are walking through a never ending commercial for Heaven and enjoying every moment of it.

murrrrrrrrrrrr..........murrrrrr...........murrrrrrrrrrrr..........murrrrrrrrrrr........
murrrrrrrrrrrr..........murrrrrr...........

Charon speaks to the shade, breaking it out of its fascination of the plains. "There will be a dock after we pass through the cave, where you will be permitted to leave this craft. On the top step, you will find a cup that you can use to drink the water from the river out of the flowing spigot next to it".

murrrrrrrrrrrr..........murrrrrr...........murrrrrrrrrrrr..........murrrrrrrrrrr........
murrrrrrrrrrrr..........murrrrrr...........

"If we're supposed to come here just to be reborn, then why are there so many people here, smelling flowers and walking barefoot in the grass?" asks the Shade hastily.

murrrrrrrrrrrr..........murrrrrr...........murrrrrrrrrrrr..........murrrrrrrrrrr........
murrrrrrrrrrrr..........murrrrrr...........

"These souls have chosen to remain here as long as they wish to keep reliving their former lives, until they are satisfied with the memories, then drink of the forgetful waters to continue their soul's voyage" Charon counters.

murrrrrrrrrrrr..........murrrrrr...........murrrrrrrrrrrr..........murrrrrrrrrrr........
murrrrrrrrrrrr..........murrrrrr...........

"You mean I can choose to be reborn or stay here for a while? Why didn't you say this before?"

murrrrrrrrrrr..........murrrrrr...........murrrrrrrrrrr..........murrrrrrrrrrr........
murrrrrrrrrrr..........murrrrrr...........

"It is because some souls want to experience life as soon as they can, never to relive the memories, only the desire to experience the joys of the flesh again" Charon says as a matter of truth. The boatman continues "You have the identical option to either stay or experience your life again. Your body was young and eliminated very early before you were able to acquire a good number of these emotions. I merely presumed you would want to practice it again".

"Again?!? How many times have I done this?" Asks the exhausted Shade.

"Many" the ferryman responds.

murrrrrrrrrrr..........murrrrrr...........murrrrrrrrrrr..........murrrrrrrrrrr........
murrrrrrrrrrr..........murrrrrr...........

As the boat reaches the mouth of the cave, the Shade begins to slouch a bit succumbing to the god of sleep. The cave has smooth walls appearing as if they have been carved by the world's most perfect drill, which produces the finest echo ever to be heard. This created the murmuring that was heard while they approached the cave.

murrrrrrrrrrr..........murrrrrr...........murrrrrrrrrrr..........murrrrrrrrrrr........
murrrrrrrrrrr..........murrrrrr...........

Now that they have traveled to what appears to be the very center of the cave, the murmuring's volume still hasn't increased. The Shade is nearly asleep when they can see a soft light peeking through the right side of the cave wall ahead of them. The Shade sees this but it barely registers due to delight of his slumber. The ferryman continues to steer them towards the ambient light while his cargo rests.

murrrrrrrrrrr………..murrrrrr………..murrrrrrrrrrr……….murrrrrrrrrr……..
murrrrrrrrrrr………..murrrrrr………..

"Arise shadow, we are nearing your egress" Charon says to his fare. And as the Shade stirs, it notices that the soft murmuring as subsided and barely has time to awaken, when they bump into the dock bathed in a background of soft bright light. The soul of a woman appears from the side wall at the foot of the steps to help the Shade out of the ferry which the Shade accepts.

As the Shade grasps her gentle hand, its own right hand begins to emerge from the silhouette in the boat. More of the Shade is seen as the left foot breaks the plane of the boat and fully stepping onto the dock revealing the soul of Dave Van Hoffman. As Dave looks at his hands and feet he drops to the dock, overwhelmed by the flood of memories that attack his mind: the love of his parents and grandparents, the friends he had, the games he played, the comic books he read, the women he liked and the woman he loved at the end; completely understanding his life and the circumstances of his death in an instant.

The woman steps near and helps him to his feet. As he stands, he glances back at the boatman and is awestruck to find that he is no longer a gruesome fearful creature, but a tired, wrinkled old man with kind bright eyes and a soft smile coming over his face.

"Welcome to the Elysian Fields" the woman says to Dave as she begins to escort him up the steps to the cup. A smile creeps across Dave's face and he turns back to Charon and asks him one last question.

"What should I do with my next life?"

"Enjoy it". And with that the ferryman pushes away from the dock to taxi his next awaiting passengers.

Brian Grall

EPILOGUE
Hell Is A Lot Like Living On Earth

As Number One races around the corner into the alley with the pack of smokes in his pocket and the shopping bags of money, he sees his partner sitting in the car, smoking.

He jumps in and shouts "Let's get outta here man!" The big man is sweating on this cold night and still gasping for air from the fever of his initiation.

"I did it, man; I did it. I shot the dude square in the face! He had no idea it was coming! I was great! I was cool! You shudda seen it!" Number Two looks over at him quickly, giving him a sly smile.

As the car peels out of the alley turning right onto Villard Avenue, the thugs hoot and holler during the drive back to their hole-in-the-wall. Number One is feeling cocky and says, "This is the best day of my life man and you didn't help me at all. Not that I needed it anyways! I just went in there like we talked and made 'dat fool do the work for me!"

"What'd you got?" Says Number Two, curiously.

"I got 'bout a thou and some rolled coin, just like he said was in 'nere and a pack of smokes" Number One says even more boastfully.

Number Two then slams his hand on the steering wheel and yells, "You stupid idiot! We're 'sposd ta git the drugs on the shelf man so we can ship 'em to our guy in The City! Damn we're dead man!"

Number One just sits frozen in his seat staring at the road ahead,

49

not even blinking.

"Hey man, let's go back and hit it real quick, so at least we get somthin'" Number One says hopefully.

"What're you stupid? We can't go back now, the cops'll be all over 'dat place bitch!" Shouts Number Two in a manner that proves to him just how stupid Number One really is. Other than the blaring rap music and the sounds of the street, the rest of the drive to their hole is silent.

Their car pulls into the driveway of their hole; Numbers Two and One get out of the car and enter the hideout, carrying their night's work. Dogs are barking somewhere not far away in the cold night.

Passing the guards, they open the doors hearing the usual 'creak' that accompanies it and move towards the room where the head of their gang is. He is listening to earsplitting music and watching TV while one of his 'girls' rubs his shoulders down his chest, in a way that means they should be in an entirely different room.

The Head is a big, muscle-bound man wearing a white t-shirt, gold chains around his neck and big dark sunglasses, barely concealing the slash marks on his upper left cheek that he received in a knife fight three years before when he took this gang from the previous Head. His reward for killing the former Head was that slash and a vacant left eye.

As The Head has his own head lying back in the half-exposed bosom of his woman, he watches from under his glasses as his two men step in front of him and says in a voice that was surprisingly upbeat, "What'd you score?"

Number One responds "A grand, some rolled coin and smokes", hoping to leech off the positive attitude The Head was in. This positive attitude didn't last long. The music shuts off.

"What you mean only a grand and some smokes? Where's the rest of the money in the bottom of the safe? You bitches were supposed to get the whole damn thing!"

"The manager couldn't get us in the bottom, so we took what was on top! He said the only way he could get it open was with a key from the armored truck guys! Honest, I wouldn't lie to you man!" Number One shouts in a completely panicked tone.

A moment passes as The Head looks at Number Two for some kind of sign, which never comes. "I send you out to get the drugs and some cash and you come back with not even half of what I asked for!?! What were you idiots thinking!?! Now I gotta get some more drugs somewhere and send them to The Director and explain this screw-up! Believe me, heads will roll!" says The Head in a very heated tone.

"Whose idea was this to follow through?" asks the Head. Number Two raises his head with a sneer on his lips and in his voice and says, "It was his, boss. He just wanted me to drive so he could show you he was ready to join up".

"Oh, so you're a big man now, huh? Wanna do everything by yo'self?" The Head looks back at Number Two and says, "Take his ass down to the Boo Box and let the dogs have him. I can't stand a man who thinks he can do a job by his'self with no idea of the circumstances if he fails. Get this chump outta my face!"

"No! You gotta believe me, I can do it right, give me another chance! No! You can't do this to me, I'm your cousin man! You can't do this to me!" cries Number One while he falls to his knees trying to fight being dragged from the room.

Smiling, Number Two grabs his gun from his back, kneels down next to him, sticks it behind Number One's skull and tells him "I've been wanting to do this a long time" as he and others pick Number One up and walk him through the hallway, to the first door on their left and down into the basement where the dogs can be heard growling.

Number One continues to beg for his life and for a second chance but it falls on deaf ears. The only thing these men want to hear is the sound of animals ripping the flesh from his bones and the screams he'll make. These are the select men that clean up the mess that's left behind when someone screws up and they enjoy their job to the fullest; the Cleaners. Part of their job is to make sure that the dogs are fed once every few days, just for times such as this. This insures that the dogs will decimate their prey.

Number Two leads the group to the door, opens and holds it for the soon-to-be-departed and his entourage. Number One continues to scream as he's tossed down the stairs like a dirty towel headed for the laundry. As he smacks against the cinder block wall at the bottom, he hears the dogs begin to bark uncontrollably, smelling the fresh blood pouring from his face. He staggers to his feet, clutching his hurt left arm and wields around trying to find a final way out of this.

Number One sees the basement and now he understands what the last victim was thinking when he was down here before – hate. He sees the half-darkened room with the main arena being the only part that's well lit, for the carnage. He sees a bunch of support pillars with various tools hanging on them, a large circular key ring near the cellar door where the dogs are let out into the yard to move, but no more than two at a time. He also sees the cage in front of him where he will make his last stand. Around the upper interior walls of the sound proof Boo Box are a row of narrow windows that look out into the yard. Number Two spots a shadow that resembles a man or a tree just outside the glass and shouts for help, praying he's heard.

At this point, the rest of the Cleaners come down in good spirits and money in hand, ready to bet on how long he lasts against the dogs. Going bet is up to five thousand for three minutes and climbs to seven thousand when its time.

As the gate's unlocked and Number One's pushed into the arena, he desperately looks up once more at that windowpane when he's struck by the first dog, then the second, third and fourth; tearing at him from all directions, ripping tendons and shredding him like scraping the paint off the siding of your house. Number One is screaming and reeling in pain, trying to fight off the crazed dogs, but that just makes them that much hungrier. One of the dogs gets through his pitifully protecting hands to his head and latches onto his nose, pulling it from his face.

The Cleaners are cheering, throwing their fists into the air, the closer ones getting sprayed with flecks of blood and flesh. In his last seconds of consciousness, he glimpses up one last time and still sees the shadow that looks like a man or a tree.

Except this time the tree moves ever so slightly, as flaming white eyes shine at Number One and whispers in a delightfully morose voice, "I'll see you soon" then fades into the blackness of the night.

Author Stats

REAL NAME: *Brian Grall*
KNOWN ALIASES: *Grall, The Professor, Gralsh, Daddy*
DUAL IDENTITY: *Publicly known only to him*
BASE OF OPERATIONS: *Space Sector 2814; currently Earth; North American continent; the United States of America; Menomonee Falls, WI; the Swamp*
CURRENT OCCUPATION: *Stay-home-dad, daydreamer, worldwide known author (as long as the world is his house)*
FORMER OCCUPATIONS: *Fanboy, daydreamer, salesman*
PLACE OF BIRTH: *Escanaba, MI – da U.P. eh?*
MARITAL STATUS: *Condemned to a life of perpetual happiness*
CURRENT GROUP MEMBERSHIP: *the Milwaukee Indians Baseball team, the Justice League of America (honorary member)*
SUPERHUMAN POWERS: *Mutant ability to tear through two dozen long boxes of comics in an hour*
SOURCE OF POWERS: *Brain aneurysm, located in the 'Bats in the Belfry' epicenter*
SPECIAL SKILLS: *Ability to read comics, diaper changing, drawing, can 'zone out' during football games, TV shows and commercials*
WEAPONS: *Shotgun mouth, rapier wit, 84 MPH fastball*
FIRST APPEARANCE: *April, 1976*

Acheron: The Stream of Woe

(dedication continued)

Ahem...*his beautiful and wonderfully understanding wife Debbie; his daughter Emma for keeping him young and being his greatest creation; his dog Indy ("we named the dog, Indiana!"); his parents for buying him so many toys to help his imagination soar with no siblings to break them or get in the way; his friends that still dare to be called his friends; his cousins Tom and Bob for continuing to act as they did when they were kids; alternate universes; the third person narrative; his favorite non-picture book author Douglas Adams; flannel; Escanaba and da U.P eh?; MARCO!; Scribbles; his ability to draw and customize action figures; POLO!; The Guild of Calamitous Intent; time travel; Captain James Tiberius Kirk (for obvious reasons); the Big Bang (which is widely considered a bad move); movies; the BTC; cows; waffles; Sir Arthur Guinness for the greatest beverage in the known universe (outside of the Pan Galactic Gargle Blaster); the U.S. Postal Service; Fuddruckers; Nicolas Cage for not portraying Superman; Matt Stone and Trey Parker; riding lawnmowers; building snow forts; baseball; the Green Bay Packers; Walt Disney; Joe Shuster/Jerry Siegel and Superman; Bob Kane and Batman; William Moulton Marston and Wonder Woman; Ben Edlund and the Tick; Stan Lee and your friendly neighborhood Spider-Man as well as the thousands of other comic books he's read over the years and Matt Damon – "Maaatt Daaamon".*

Assassin Insurrection

Michelle Johnston

You ever have one of those days where it seems like the world has it out for you? I get them all the time. Today, however, was taking the cake.

If I had to spend one more hour hiding under the bathroom sink I was going to lose it. It wasn't unheard of for a Scout to have to lie low, but this was getting ridiculous. Despite being a petite woman, I was twisted like a contortionist. My muscles were on fire. The target I was scouting had unexpectedly come home. Listening to him move around convinced me that he likely always came home at this time. Zeus had given me bad intel.

Zeus was a thorn in my side. He seemed to think he was *the* Zeus, the ancient god of some culture long gone. Even though our identities were kept anonymous during communications by the small implants near our ears, I could tell he was blustery and a stickler for perfection. He was the reason I was in this predicament in the first place. As my Overseer, he passed down the contracts from the higher-ups, assigning them to a specific unit. He had initiated contact this morning with the name of a new target and told me the condo would be vacant all day. But now here I was, stuck in a cabinet. Phoenix would not be happy about this.

The other half of my unit, Phoenix, was an accomplished Assassin with over one hundred and fifty hits over the course of six years. He, or at least I assumed he was a he, specialized in the more lucrative rush jobs. He needed his Scout to turn around enough information in one day to enable him to finish the contract in time.

Unfortunately I was trapped under a sink, about to miss my

deadline without a single piece of useful intelligence. This was my fifth job as his Scout, and I was quickly learning why no one else had wanted to be the replacement for his last Scout. I could already guess how our communication would go tonight. Failure of any kind was not acceptable to Phoenix. I sent up a small prayer, thankful that he couldn't know my identity. I wouldn't have to worry about him coming to my door and harassing me.

Finally I heard the target head to bed. Soon I'd be able to make my escape and deliver my information, or lack of it, to Phoenix.

***

The first thing I did when I got home was dial up a big bowl of ice cream on my synthfood dispenser. More so than alcohol, ice cream could soothe a frazzled confidence and dull the pain of failure. I definitely needed some dulling before contacting Phoenix. Three bowls later I gathered enough courage to make the call.

I instructed my CommSys to connect me to the virtual meeting room Phoenix and I used to communicate. It was thirteen agonizing minutes before a mechanized voice informed me he was arriving. Just like him to let me squirm.

"Swan, why haven't you sent over your report?" He sounded mildly curious, never a good sign. Curiosity from Phoenix was like a cat scrutinizing a mouse.

"Zeus told me the condo would be empty all day. The target came home as soon as I got there. I tried my best. I was trapped in the condo for hours."

"Is this a joke?" He let out a slow, barely controlled breath, and I felt the ice cream turn to rock in my stomach. "No, I don't think you're capable of joking. I'm not even sure what you *are* capable of at this point."

Silence hovered between us, and I tried not to sound as helpless as I felt. "I really did try, Phoenix. Sometimes things don't go to plan." Did that come across as begging for forgiveness? Oh, who was I kidding. I was begging. I needed to keep this job.

His voice dripped with sarcasm. "Things always go to schedule when a well thought out plan is in place. Obviously you had no contingency plan. I thought I was working with a professional Scout." Clearly forgiveness was not to be had.

"I..."

"We'll deal with this later. I have...business...to attend to. I guess I'll be handling this job without a Scout."

His quick dismissal stung more than anything he'd said. The CommSys informed me his connection had terminated, and I dialed up more ice cream.

***

I had just fallen asleep when my CommSys jolted me back awake. I squinted at my clock and realized it was well past midnight. I'd spent more time wallowing in front of the vidscreen watching re-runs than I'd realized.

The blinking light on the CommSys indicated two unread messages. The first was a rather scathing message from Zeus outlining the standards for contract fulfillment. It included a few subtle references to the Scouts that had filled this job before me. Apparently Phoenix had already forwarded my failure to our Overseer. The second message was from Phoenix himself.

Incoming message
Sender: Phoenix
Body: How goes the brooding?

You've got to be kidding. Why was he messaging me in the middle of the night? I knew he wasn't the type to comfort or empathize with others. Surely he was only trying to make it worse. Trying not to let him know how bad it had really been, I sent back a reply.

It sucks that a mistake like that happened. But brooding won't help.

It seems your synthfood dispenser and vidscreen would say otherwise.

Okay now he was getting creepy. But I was pretty sure I'd let slip to him that I was female. And what girl didn't run for the food and vidscreen after a rough day? I told him as much.

Funny. But it will take more than that to scare me. You're just using stereotypes to increase the probability of being right.

Probability is unnecessary. Let's talk details. You live in Benpark Row, the seediest part of town you can find without druggies or gang bangers. You feel more comfortable around people who live in squalor. Successful people threaten you because you know you will never be good enough in their eyes. You'd like to move elsewhere but you've made that condo feel like home and home is the one thing you never had growing up.

I was stunned. How could he know this? Regardless of whether or not his reasoning about my motives was true (and I fervently told myself that it wasn't) he knew exactly where I lived. My heart raced and I cringed when he sent another message.

I'll take it from your silence that you've come to appreciate the position I have you in. Now that we've established that I do know who and where you are, you can think about what that means for your future after a performance like today's. Sweet dreams.

I was so tired of trying to prove myself to Phoenix on the last few jobs. No wonder he had gone through so many Scouts before me. With his knowledge of me, he had altered the balance of power firmly in his direction. Well, what was preventing him from seeing me replaced? What was preventing me from doing the same thing to him? I was a Scout, information was my business. Perhaps a little blackmail would once and for all end his poor treatment of me. I made a resolution to be brave and follow through with my new plan to even the scales.

Since I couldn't really sleep after my chat with Phoenix, I put myself to work. Data-mining was a demanding task but Benpark Row always quieted down after the bars closed. I could expect to have at least a few hours of full concentration without distractions.

By the time the sun was warming my toes, I was ready to give up. I could find fleeting bits of information, but nothing that painted any picture or pattern of where Phoenix could be. I was not giving up just yet. Scouting the rush jobs had forced me to develop new avenues of digging up information. It would cost me, but it could cost me more if I couldn't turn up anything on Phoenix.

***

After promising more money than I should have, I had finally found a lead on Phoenix, and a good one at that. One of my contacts admitted he had info on someone whom Phoenix used to work with. The hit to my bank account would be worth it to get out from under Phoenix's thumb. I glanced down at my car's autopilot. I should get there before sundown, but just barely.

***

I had the car park itself at the start of the forest, about a mile from the house where the contact lived. The electrical power lines running across the land toward the sunset looked like something out of a history book. How we humans ever lived so primitively was beyond me.

Damaging my ride on the washed out road would only bring the wrath of Zeus upon me, and I already had enough of that as it was. I'd hoof it the rest of the way.

An old cabin appeared through the trees. I caught a glimpse of water, a dock and a ramshackle boat. How quaint. My contact was turning out to be a more interesting character than I'd thought.

No lights were on and my knock at the door went unanswered. The door was locked with a surprisingly new lock, at least the owner had bothered to put in some modern security. A quick peer through the front window showed a typical rustic cabin kitchen. It boasted an electric stove, refrigerator, and a small table with some chairs. Some rusty knives lay strewn haphazardly across the counter. None of it looked like it had been used in centuries.

I needed to figure out what game my informant thought he was playing. It seemed unlikely that he lived here now. But, I came all the way out here and I wasn't leaving until I got some information. No more timid Swan, I'd show Phoenix that two could play his game.

The old building actually had hinges and a handle on its doors. Those old-world hunting types really went all out in authenticity. I reached into a pocket and pulled out a las-blade. It wasn't strictly legal so I kept it hidden on my person. I'd been itching to try it out since I'd bought it on a trip to one of the border cities a few weeks ago. The man I'd bought it from swore it would slice through almost any type of alloy. Brass hinges should melt like butter.

A full minute later the hinges barely had a scratch. Not brass after all. Curious. I don't like curious. It never boded well.

I looked around and noticed an old footpath going down to the dock. My fear told me to just get out of there, but I decided checking out the boat first couldn't do any harm. I was all in at this point.

The inside of the boat was littered with photos. My muscles tensed as I picked one up. It was a photo of the first woman I'd scouted for Phoenix. Another showed a man I'd scouted just last week.

Dizzy from shock, I stumbled back onto the dock. A trail of wet footprints led away from the boat. Those weren't there when I'd climbed into the boat. I began to wonder if I was ever really meant to meet a contact here. My heart rate skyrocketed as I heard a beeping noise. It was just my CommSys. Pull it together, Swan.

Incoming message
Sender: Phoenix
Body: Enjoying your day off? On my days off I like to
relax on the lake.

My head snapped up as a form appeared on the end of the dock, blocking my only route out.

"Hello, Swan. How does it feel to be out-scouted?"

I gasped in disbelief. "Phoenix?"

"How...interesting...to find you here..."

He continued to talk, but I couldn't hear him over the blood pounding in my head. My mind frantically ran through options. I could jump in the water, and try to swim away. But where would I go? The boat didn't look like it even ran. Taser. I always carried a taser just in case.

Without even realizing, my hand had already pulled it out and pointed it toward him. It felt like a dream as the wires shot out. His mouth opened in an "O" of surprise and he crumpled to the dock. Reality came storming back and I took off running.

The tree branches stung as they whipped my face and arms.

How far away had I parked? A noise at my heels startled me and as I tried to look behind I tripped and fell hard. I lay on the ground panting, spitting out mossy earth. The taste made me cringe. I lay still and listened for any noise. Nothing. Picking myself up, I began to make my way back to the car as quickly and quietly as I could.

Just as the the edge of the forest came in sight, a great weight landed on top of me and I collapsed. Being slammed between Phoenix and the ground knocked the wind out of me. I struggled but ultimately his strength won out. Grabbing my hair, he literally dragged me over to the vehicle.

He pulled me up and slammed me against the car door. The only thing I could do to defend myself was pull a pen out of my pocket, brandishing it wildly.

"That's it?" he laughed scornfully. "From taser to pen? I thought we already talked about having a contingency plan." He shook his head. "I'm not surprised, though. You're a Scout. You're weak."

In a move I'd seen in martial arts flicks as a kid, he twisted it out of my hand. Before I could move he'd grabbed his pistol and pointed it at my head. Then he nodded toward the car.

"Get in."

Still dazed, I opened the driver door and climbed in. He got in the passenger seat, still pointing his weapon at me.

"Drive back to the cabin."

"It won't make it over this road," I protested.

"Shut up and do it. Now we can finish the conversation we started on the dock."

As I drove toward the cabin he began to talk and my heart sunk at what he said. I knew I'd been played.

"You know I had no idea who you were. I wouldn't have been able to find you if you weren't so predictable, tracking me, bringing yourself out in the open." He smiled knowingly at the look of shock in my eyes. "You were so easy to read. It was a sure bet to guess about where you lived and what you did in your spare time. If I'd have known how right I was, I'd have kept going. Maybe talked about your family."

He had me park next to the cabin and he led me in, still at gunpoint. In the back corner of the kitchen were two hooks in the ceiling. A man hung from one and I could only assume it was my contact. A spasm shot through my body as an image of myself hanging next to him flew through my mind. Without thinking I lunged for one of the knives I'd seen earlier on the table.

He deftly stepped in my way, blocking my access to the table. "Those are my toys, not yours. But don't worry, I have something different in mind for you."

"Why are you doing this?"

The question seemed to catch him off guard. He paused as a blank look came over his face.

"Why should I have to share the credit for my hits? All the glory goes to you and your *impeccable* scouting," he sneered. "I've proven that I don't need you or your information. But enough talk. It's time to finish this."

Reaching into his back pocket, he pulled out a syrin-press and advanced toward me. I had never seen one in real life. Breaking-edge technology and highly illegal, not even medical staff used them. Word had it that they injected liquids with a blast of air that parted the cells of your skin. No needles necessary. It was just the thing I would expect an Assassin to carry. Whatever he planned on drugging me with couldn't be good. My taser had been the only weapon I carried, and it was lying somewhere on the dock. Time seemed to slow as I backed away, feeling utterly defenseless.

Think, you're a Scout! Resourceful is your middle name. Becca actually, but it should have been Resourceful. I knew my resolution to be brave was being tested and I had no intention of failing.

Frantically I searched my pockets for anything of use. Of course, my las-blade! I grabbed it and turned it on as I brought it out of my pocket, aiming for his head. The laser left a gash across his cheek and then flashed into his eyes. With a cry of pain, he instinctively brought his hands to his face, and tagged himself with the syrin-press in the process.

Whatever fleeting time I bought myself expired as he let out an agonizing scream and grabbed for me. Backing away, I barely escaped his grasp and tripped over a chair, my las-blade flying out of my hands. I fell through the air, unable to change direction, and watched horrified as he lunged toward me. Kicking at him wildly, I had the wry wish that I was the type to wear high heels. Then we collided as we hit the ground and he latched onto my throat. I tried in vain to slap at his head, but I had no leverage and my fists barely made him grunt. His face contorted in rage and his grip tightened.

My vision started to blur and the edges filled with sand. So this is what it feels like to die. And just when I had finally found the courage to take control of my life. The only thing still visible was Phoenix's face. Why was he the last thing I got to see?

***

Gradually I realized I was staring at the ceiling gasping, with Phoenix laying next to me. Whatever was in that syrin-press must have finally decided to kick in.

His breathing was slow and intermittent. Apparently he wanted me unconscious but not dead. At least not yet. Bending down, I picked up his gun. If I had learned anything, it's that you can never be too careful. Especially around Assassins.

A faint beeping noise grabbed my attention. His CommSys was buzzing. Interesting. Discarding my own, I pulled his off his head. A few quick modifications and it fit to my own ear and eye like a glove.

"Hello?" I answered.

"Phoenix, this is Zeus. I need confirmation of the kill."

An image of a contract popped into view. The target's vitals flashed and I felt nauseous.

Name: unknown
Alias: Swan
Occupation: Scout
Location: present whereabouts unconfirmed
Bounty: 20,000 Crane

Pointing the gun at Phoenix's head, I smiled as a new opportunity opened before me.

"Confirmed." Hesitating slightly, I gathered the courage and nodded to myself. My finger tightened on the trigger. "I'm going to need a new scout."

Michelle Johnston

Michelle Johnston is an avid reader and avoider of all things meat. She spends her time bicycling, cooking, and day dreaming. When not doing these things she does what any other self respecting woman does: lavishes her love on her cat...and her husband.

Michelle Johnston

The Accident

Matthew J. Kolell

The Accident

"This is Detective James Dobrowski. We're in interview room two of the Safety building. It's 12:56 pm on Tuesday April 22 and I'm here with... What's your name?"

"Daniel Britton."

"With Daniel Britton. Is there anything I can get you before we start, something to eat or drink, a cigarette?"

"I'd like a Whopper extra large value meal with a Coke. I didn't get to have lunch before you picked me up."

"Okay. I'm going to step out for a minute then to have somebody pick that up for you."

***

He sits back down with that obnoxious smirk on his face like he's going to get me to talk about whatever he wants me to, either by breaking or befriending me. Personally, I think he looks pretty pathetic with his gut hanging over his belt, that has his badge and Glock attached to it. Probably thinks he's all that because he doesn't have to wear a uniform but still gets to walk around with a gun at his side.

Name? Date of birth? Parents names? Brother and sisters names? Children? Married? What's the point of all these questions? Probably to be sure I'm really who I say I am. I don't know though. I've never been arrested. Only have 2 speeding tickets and that was when I was 19. Never really had much contact with authorities but then I've been avoiding them for the last 14 years.

***

Knock, knock, knock.

An officer holding my drink and food was at the door. The detective waved for her to come in as I finished up with my speeding ticket stories.

"Your food's here. I take it you'd rather eat while continuing this discussion instead of waiting until we're done."

"Yes," I responded. Just another way of showing me who's in charge. Either eat while we talk or get cold food if I don't, and if I don't cooperate, maybe none at all, except for their legendary bologna sandwich and water.

The aroma of the flame broiled burger penetrated my nostrils as she brought the bag in. Crap, I forgot to get it with cheese! As I opened the bag the smell hit me harder, the burger and fries made me realize just how hungry I was. I hadn't even eaten breakfast this morning.

"Okay, where were we?" the detective continued as I laid the food out. "That's the last contact you've had with any officers or any other type of law enforcement."

"Yes sir," I replied, continuing the illusion that I respected his authority. Raising the burger to my mouth, I smelled deeply. I could taste the burger even before it got to my mouth- the warm meat, the onions, hint of tomato and... What is that smell? The delicate bouquet of orchids and jasmine? In my burger? Continuing to chew, I took a few more whiffs. Definitely not from my food. Maybe from the officer? No, not her either; she wasn't the type to wear that scent. It was coming from the detective I realized, as I dumbly stared at him, mouth open forgetting to chew.

76

The Accident

"Is there something wrong?' he asked.

"No. I just realized I forgot to order with cheese and no pickles. I hate how you bite into a pickle without realizing they're there." I think I did pretty well covering it up. I think I was so nervous at first that I never realized any odor until the food came. It wasn't so strong that he put it on himself but must have gotten it rubbed off on him recently. I looked him over again as I sipped my soda. Probably a nooner. He's too old for his wife to wear that, most likely a mistress or call girl. Sizing him up again, I asked, "How long have you been married?"

Catching him a little off guard, he stammered, "That's not what we're here to talk about right now."

"It's nice to have someone you can come home to after a long day's work. Someone who loves and trusts you. A person you can share everything with and know that you'll always be faithful to each other. I haven't had that for the last 14 years." I could tell by his reaction that I was right on target with the cheating and threw in the last part to get him back on track.

"Speaking of 14 years ago, why don't you tell me what happened."

Then it hit me. She smelled like that. Fourteen years ago, the memories came rushing back like it was only hours ago.

***

"What the hell are you still doing in front of the TV. Its almost 11 and you're still not dressed. I can't believe you still watch cartoons. Are you going to grow up and get some work done around here? I've been up cleaning since 8."

She was wearing her tight red v-neck t-shirt and black skirt.

She looked awesome in that outfit and she knew it turned me on. I could tell from the outline, she had her VS matching lace bra and thong on. Her smooth, sensual curves were evident underneath her clothing.

"I'll get going and start work outside after I get in the shower. Unless you want to give me a little motivation to get me going."

"How late were you up playing those games last night? Maybe you should have come to bed then and got some. It's a beautiful spring morning and I wanted to do some shopping with you later today. That's why I got my work started so early. You know me, work first then play. Except I don't stay up all hours playing games when there's house work that has to be done the next day."

"Okay, I'm going," I said, as I got off the coach.

"You'll probably want to take a nap after lunch and we'll never get anything done that I wanted and we'll waste a totally free day away. So don't even ask."

There were two reasons for her to wear that outfit. The first was that she wanted me and knew she could turn me on and get me to do work, or whatever, done that day before we had some fun. Or she was mad at me and wanted to punish me. You messed up and look what you have right in front of you but you're too selfish to get your lazy ass out of bed and do what I expect out of you. I started to realize that this was going to be a day where it was the second of those options.

Standing in the the shower, I could still picture her and how hot she looked. How she would slowly take off her clothes in front of me showing off her nearly naked body, teasing me. I thought I could please myself because there was little chance I was getting anything from her today. But I was actually still too pissed at her.

After I got dressed and walked downstairs, she asked, "Can

you help me to put up the shelves and pictures on the wall now?"

"I was going to change the oil and mow the lawn outside. You can do those things without me."

"But I want your opinion of where to put them."

"It'll be fine wherever they go but its already been 45 hundred miles."

"You could have done that this morning!" she yelled. "You keep putting stuff off and when I ask you for help, that's when you want to do it. Then you complain about how something looks or how you don't like something after its up. You don't help out around the house and I work as many hours as you do but you still expect me to cook and clean and pick up after you."

"Well you don't always pick up after yourself either," I roared back. "But I pick things up that you leave lying around, its called working together as a team. You can ask for help instead of expecting me to do something. I can't read your mind. And I couldn't mow the lawn this morning, you know the neighbors complain if we do anything loud before 11."

"Then you should have helped me this morning with it but you were up until all hours of the morning …."

Let me explain something about our neighborhood. Its made up of small starter homes where there are either young people just starting out in home ownership or older people conserving their money and not really needing a bigger home any more. So except for the odd baby here and there, there weren't any kids running around. The young couples could go out downtown to be loud and have fun and the odd outburst late at night wouldn't usually be enough to wake up the old folks. So it was a pretty quiet neighborhood with the houses stacked on top of each other. To top it off, we were surrounded by old people, who had nothing better to do than to pry into others' business and gossip about it when they had the chance. The young ones gave them more fodder but they were merciless on their peers if something juicy came up. So needless to say, our argument wasn't just between us. But Bob and Laverne and Melvin and Dorthea and who knows who else.

***

Just then a man in a black suit and tie with a white shirt entered the room. "I'm special agent Kyle Brady. I talked to you about an hour ago. You're detective James Dobrowski, I presume, and this would be the suspect."

It wasn't a question, it was a statement of fact. But he was really dressed like that, it was a surreal moment like something out of a movie. It was obvious who was now going to be in charge of the questioning. Along with him came the odor of motor oil, grease and hand-soap.

"I would have been here sooner but I had some problems with the vehicle. I would like to talk with you a moment before we continue the discussion with Mr. Britton."

"Sure thing. Glad to meet you agent Brady," the detective said. He held out his hand to shake the agent's hand but it just hung there. Agent Brady held up his perfectly manicured hands stating, "I washed them but I think it best to not shake your hand as I can still feel the oil on them."

As they walked out of the room, the scent of the oil still lingered sending me back into my reverie.

***

I threw the wrench on the garage floor still mad from earlier. I looked up as I tried wiping the grime from my hands and saw her storming towards me. Oh great, I thought, what does she want now?

The Accident

"Are you done changing the oil yet?" she screamed. "I need to use the car. Obviously you're not ready even though I told you I wanted to leave at 4. Now you'll just have to deal with whatever I get and if you complain, we'll see if you get some anytime soon."

By then she was in the garage and in my face. As I started to yell, "What the f," her hand clamped over my mouth as she grabbed my wrist and placed it on her hip. She whispered, "Feel this."

I placed my other hand on her hip and could immediately feel that her thong was no longer on.

She bent in close, "Thanks for helping me hang things inside even though I knew you were mad at me and didn't feel like doing that. I want to show you how much I appreciate that. Now lets give those old folks something to talk about." Her tongue flicked at my ear before leaning back out and yelling, "don't touch me!"

I had my hands all over her. Groping her chest, caressing her neck and running my hands through her hair. Her shirt got ripped. I would have regretted that. She looked so hot in that shirt.

She continued screaming out and I chimed in too with a few, "I'll show you whats good for you," "You'll do what I tell you to do," and "If I ever catch you cheating, I'll kick your ass."

That's when I think she said something about my friend and her. That's the only part that's fuzzy, everything else is clear as day. I was just so caught up in the moment with passion. I had her back against the wood cabinet with her legs wrapped around me. I was so into her and the way her body was responding to me. She was screaming how much she hated me while her body was showing how much she loved me and needed me. Her back was banging against the door and that's when it happened. I picked up the sound of a distant siren and at the same instant the large planter filled with soil resting on top of the cabinet fell, hitting her square on the head.

81

Blood was everywhere. There was nothing I could have done to save her. For five seconds I just held her crying. Then the scene registered in my brain, taking in everything in less than a second, like your life flashing before your eyes before you die. The fighting, yelling and sounds coming from the garage and from earlier in the day, all painted a clear picture of guilt. I panicked and knew there was no way any one would believe me, not even creating a reasonable doubt.

Ever since then I've been on the "run." But I never forgot her, I never quit loving her. I would always visit her every year on the date I proposed to her. I was paranoid someone would be watching her grave on her birthday or our anniversary. I wish there was some way I could bring her back. Never before had elation turned to despair so quickly for me. I would do anything to feel like that again.

***

"So that's your story?" the detective interrupted.

He startled me out of my trance, I had no idea when they came back in. All I could say is, "Yes."

"What about the other 28 women we've linked you to? You have a story for those too?" agent Brady asked.

"Oh those. They were all intentional," I answered with a smile.

They stood there completely dumbfounded as I finished the last of my Whopper.

The Accident

Matthew Kolell is not a best-selling author nor an award winning novelist. He does own a small business and enjoys gaming, bicycling, drinking Mountain Dew and spending time with his family. He lives in the Fox River Valley with his wife Sara, three sons, a beautiful daughter, a tall dining room table and their dog Ajax, a Great Dane mix.

Whisper

Marcus Maichle

Whisper

What follows is a fairy tale, for its hero, as it were, is quite literally a fairy. However, it is unlike the fairy tales you were told as a child. Fairies are forces of nature, given form by our thoughts and imagination. They are tied to the land and the seasons, from which many fairies draw great powers. Although immortal, most fairies fade into and out of being from the raw essence of Nature, with misty recollections of their past existences. Although fairies can exist without mankind's interference, we do have an effect on them. We use words and give things names. Words have power, and names are powerful words. Fairies can speak, and use names, but it is through the imaginations of men, women, and especially children that words grant fairies form and substance. This story begins when a particularly imaginative young man wandered to the forest.

Evan had ventured farther from the village than he had before, and stopped to listen. He was sure that one of his brothers would come soon to call him home. It was a week before Samhain, and he and his brothers had been working to bring in what remained to harvest. The growing season was coming to an end, and soon, in order to bring in fresh food, the men would begin to hunt. The youth was finally old enough to join the men on the hunt, and he was eager for the season to begin. This would be his chance to prove himself a man. Maybe then the other boys would leave him alone. Maybe then, others would finally notice him. Evan had come out here to see if he could discover any deer trails that he could mark.

The wind carried a spark of the fairy essence in it that afternoon. The Fae were preparing for the changing of the courts, and there was as much hustle in their realm as in the humans' preparations. Leaves were becoming brittle, and as the essence followed the wind through them, it gave voice to its anticipation through the rustling. The young man, bristling with his own anxieties, heard the voice, and was briefly startled.

"Who's there?" he called, and heard only another rustle in answer. It might have been squirrels that far up, rushing to hide their own winter stores. He stood a while longer, staring into the trees and listening to hear the voice again. But the only voice he could perceive now came from behind him, as one of his brothers had indeed come to bring him home.

"It's nearly time for dinner. What are you doing all the way out here? You didn't come all the way here to compose another one of your silly poems, did you?"

"No. I was just listening," the youth replied.

"To what?" asked the brother in a tone so loud and callous, there was nothing he could hear but his own echo and continued huffing.

Casting one more look out over the wood, the youth took a deep breath in, as though perhaps he could smell whatever was out there. As he exhaled his answer carried through the breeze.

"A whisper," he said, and turned to follow older brother, who simply headed back toward the village, shaking his head.

The energy, up in the leaves, having been given a name, began to take shape. As Evan walked farther away, Whisper leaned out of the trees as far as he could reach, watching. He could sense his connection to the forest, and knew that he was part of it, even though he had just come into existence. But of this strange creature who had called him into being, he knew only one thing. He knew he felt loss at seeing him go away.

For several days, Whisper paced the edge of the wood, hoping to see his fair young man again. Many times, he tried to follow the way the youth had followed his brother. But each time, a strong pull brought him back. Within the forest, he could move very swiftly, and he quickly became familiar with the entire area around him, the places where water could be found, the paths, dens, and nests of the various woodland animals. There were also several rings where he knew he would find others like him, but he was not quite ready to join them yet. It was toward these rings that he felt a strong pull, and he feared the others might make him stay with them, not allowing him to return to his place where he watched for the young man he so wanted to find.

But the young man had not come back to the wood, and Whisper could feel a change throughout the forest. The pull was beginning to draw him deeper inside the wood. Despite his great desire, he found it difficult to reach even the edge of the woods where he kept watch. Although he could not define what was pulling him, he knew that it drew him towards one of the greater rings he had encountered. Until then, avoiding the rings kept him from encountering any other fairies. The pull continued, and seemed to grow stronger as each day got a little bit colder. Then, for the first time since his encounter with the young man, he heard another voice.

"You there!" the voice called from within the wood. Whisper hadn't expected that. He'd still been trying to hear anything that would indicate the young man returning.

"Who's there?" Whisper asked. His voice was soft, but the trees around him rustled, repeating the question.

"Ah, I was right, you must be new," the voice answered. "Otherwise you'd know that we cannot tell others our names."

"That's silly, I'm…" Whisper started to say, but he found that the name the young man called him had slipped his mind."

"As I said," the voice returned. This time, as the voice spoke, a form began to take shape in front of Whisper. While Whisper was pale compared to the vibrant youth he'd seen, this fairy before him was paler yet. "I cannot tell you, but surely you can figure out who I am.

Have you not noticed the changes here?"

"I've noticed a pull drawing me toward the greater circles," Whisper tried.

"Yes, you would be drawn to the gathering. In fact, it's surprising that you aren't there. But I am not called 'pull.' Try again. What else have you noticed?"

"It's colder."

"Good, good. Still, you are new, and you haven't even begun to feel cold yet."

"Well it's been only days, but there's definitely been a Chill these last few."

"Ah, splendid!" the fairy exclaimed, suddenly appearing more substantial.

"I'm sorry, I don't know how to teach you my name," Whisper's eyes lowered as he spoke.

"Ha ha! No need my new friend," laughed Chill. "Here you are, this close to the mortals, your voice coming through the leaves. I've been around many seasons, and you are not the first Whisper I've met."

Whisper felt a brief surprise at the stranger speaking his name, which he suddenly remembered as it was spoken. He also suddenly felt himself more present. And although he did not notice it consciously, he stood a little more solidly, and the pull seemed to have less affect on him.

"If I am not the first, then there are others?" he inquired.

"…were," Chill corrected. "You see, mortals come out here and hear Whispers all the time, but soon forget them."

"What happens then?" asked Whisper.

"If one of us is forgotten, we fade back into the essence, until something or someone else shapes us into another being." When he'd finished speaking, Chill looked over Whisper, as a child might examine a fallen leaf he'd picked up. "If you don't mind me asking, how long have you been here stalking the edge of the wood."

"It's been some days." He answered. Instinctively, he looked to the sky, knowing that there was a reference there. "On the first night, the moon was full."

"Well, that is auspicious," Chill tilted his head and seemed to be examining Whisper closely. It made the newer fairy slightly uncomfortable, but his curiosity was stronger.

"You said that we vanish if we're forgotten," Whisper's tentative inquiry began.

"Yes, and I'll admit, counting the days since the full moon, I don't believe I've met a Whisper yet who has remained as long as you. The full moon would account for that some, but even this surprises me."

Whisper turned away from his new friend, his gaze returning to the distance where he'd seen the two brothers disappear into the distance. His mind was spinning with the information which Chill had just told him, or more precisely, reminded him of. Yes, he'd known these things somehow. *We form and reform from the essence of nature. So our history must remain with us in some sort of continuous memory.* The word "memory" echoed in his thoughts. It became very important with what he'd just heard Chill say about being forgotten, and him still being here. He turned back to the other fairy, a look of joy on his face.

"He's thinking about me! That's why I'm still here. He hasn't forgotten me!" Trees began to shake with Whisper's exclamation.

"'He'?" Chill's expression became simultaneously inquisitive and understanding. Whisper started to recall something. Other than a few glances reflected in the ever cooling waters, Whisper hadn't paid much attention to his own appearance, but he knew he appeared boyish. Usually, when mortal boys came to the wood, they imagined either pixyish girl faeries to run off with, or dangerous villains to combat. This lad had imagined Whisper, a soft voice that spoke kind words to him. It was an image that Whisper dared to call 'romantic.'

"Tell me. Do you know anything about him?"

"Very little. Other than Naming me, he spoke very little."

"Spoke? To whom?"

"Another man"

"A friend? A lover maybe?" Chill was clearly leading up to something, but Whisper felt this assessment was wrong.

"No, not a lover," he answered. Recalling how much the two looked alike, the correct word came through the mists. "His brother."

At this Chill seemed disappointed, though not so much that it hadn't been a lover, but that his answer had missed. His face twisted somewhat as he worked to come up with some other thought. It was Whisper who provided the lead.

"The brother accused him of coming all the way out here to write a poem," he said.

"He's a poet, then," Chill stated with a sense of satisfaction. The reaction sparked another memory for Whisper, something about those mortals who create things. Chill seemed about to explain the conclusion, but Whisper had reached it himself.

"He's a Dreamer." Now it made so much sense to Whisper. While not often seen as vital to mortal survival, the ability of some people to see things that don't already exist is a powerful boon to the fairies. The emotions of a creative "dreamer," especially one who passes his vision on to others in some form, can create powerful fairies indeed.

"Tell me, friend," Chill began again. "Are you expecting your Dreamer to return here? Is that why you wait here every day, resisting the pull to gather?"

"I am not sure," Whisper mused. "I have been hoping that he will."

"And that hope is what keeps you here, instead of moving through the ring?"

The ring, Whisper thought. Samhain is near. The summer court would be moving over to the fairy realm, and the winter court would be coming in for their reign of the natural world. Chill was probably one of the early emissaries of Winter.

"If you feel so strongly about it," Chill continued, "you could stay on this side. You are borne to Summer, but close enough to Samhain to stay here during Winter's reign."

"I don't have to cross?" Whisper asked, intrigued.

"Eventually, you do, but not this crossing. And it's not without risk. Warm weather and changing seasons gives humans reason to dream and think of fanciful things. But as cold weather drags on, they become more concerned with survival and practical matters. If you cross over, you would survive in the fairy realm until their thoughts and dreams come back to the joyful things. If you stay, he may become too wrapped up in surviving the winter to think of you, and then…"

"If I have a choice," said Whisper, "then I'll stay."

Having decided, Whisper turned back to his vigil which he continued to keep. He remained watching until, still with no sign of the young poet returning, Samhain had arrived.

***

It is a night of both dreams and nightmares. Among the humans, games and chicanery join morbid images and good natured fright. In the fairy wilds, ancient battles are replayed, reminders of the reason for the accords now held. In both lands, formality and tradition join with revelry and chaos.

Whisper had followed Chill to the gathering place, and allowed himself this night away from his vigil. His decision made, he knew he could join the revels and still return to his watch. And so, Whisper danced through the night. He danced with wild abandon with the last remaining Embers of summer. He spun freely in whirlwind circles with several autumn Gusts. He wove through the multitude in a great courtly number, smiling broadly at Chill each time he passed him in the great pattern he instinctively knew.

All the while, atop a shimmering dais of spun starlight, a majestic couple observed the festivities, their faces bright and warm, but seeming tired. The king and queen of the summer court had brought all of the summer fairies to this gathering in readiness for crossing. They greeted the early arrivals from Winter with courtesy, and watched the interaction between the two courts with mild interest. The complex dance before them wound to a close, and the music paused, bringing all of the dancers together facing the dais. The king stood, offering his hand to the queen, who rose to accept it. Whisper recognized that the choreography had arranged the dancers so that the summer fairies filled the half of the circle nearest the dais, while the winter fairies filled the other.

A slow processional melody began to play, and the summer king and queen descended the steps of the dais, casting their smiling looks out over the crowd. When the couple reached the lowest step of the dais, the summers parted creating an aisle leading to the crowd of winters. Then the winters parted, so that the aisle continued fully across the circle, revealing a solitary fairy. The Queen of Winter waited for the aisle to completely open before proceeding. Although fairies do not truly age, Winter queen had a much older appearance than her summer counterparts. From his vantage point, Whisper could see that her eyes were more serious, but there was still a measure of cheer in them, and she radiated the same majesty as the Summer king and queen.

They continued their processions, fairies lowering to bow as they passed. Whisper realized that where he stood was the point where the three sovereigns would meet. The fairy rulers smiled to all, somehow meeting even lowered eyes with their own. As the two processions approached, Whisper knew the exact moment, and swept himself into a bow as graceful as any of the dances he'd just performed. He sensed his act of reverence empowering the royal fairies, and in return, he felt a strong radiance fill him. Still tingling from the exchange, Whisper felt himself moving again, and realized that all of the fairies had begun to turn around the circle so that now the winters formed an aisle toward the dais, and the summers filled the opposite side. As the winter court passed across the dais, frost spread across it, and ice began to crystallize over the separate chairs upon which the king and queen had sat, forming instead a single throne of ice.

Having so far known automatically how to move, it surprised Whisper to find himself standing in a clearing where the two courts had separated from each other. The king and queen of summer turned their gazes in Whisper's direction. With the same grace as before, Whisper bowed again, but this time, as he stood, he moved toward the winter crowd. With a slightly grim understanding showing on their faces, the king and queen nodded to him, acknowledging his unspoken request to remain. Whisper then turned and bowed to the winter queen, who in turn nodded her acceptance. Then, the couples resumed their promenades, the winter queen ascending the dais to be seated at her throne, the king and queen of summer processing to the far end of the circle, where they faded away, followed by the rest of their court.

***

With Samhain past, Whisper returned to his watch at the edge of the forest. He no longer felt a force pulling him toward the fairy rings, but from time to time, Chill would persuade him to join him and other winter fairies in their various revels.

"We're part of the woods," he would explain. "We'll know if anyone approaches."

Indeed, several times in the next few days, groups of humans had come to the woods. With the onset of winter, there was nothing else for the people to harvest from their fields, and so from time to time, groups would come to the wood to hunt. Both Chill and Whisper understood that hunting was a necessity, and the relationship between these hunters and their wild home was understood. Still, they enjoyed testing the hunters. Chill could send cold bursts of wind that broke through any layers of clothing, and Whisper often used his voice to spook or mislead hunters. Those who endured these tests had a successful hunt, which the fairies respected just as they would respect a wolf succeeding in a hunt.

On one particular morning, as Whisper reclined in the high branches of a tree, he sensed yet another hunting party approach. This time, however, a familiar presence was with them. Whisper sat up suddenly, startling Chill who had been resting nearby. Seeing Whisper's reaction, Chill understood.

"Is it him?" Chill asked.

"I think so." Whisper answered. In a few short leaps, Chill was at Whispers side, poking him in the ribs. "Hey!" Whisper cried out. The wind hissed through empty branches.

"Just checking," Chill stated matter-of-factly. "Your presence is pretty strong now," he continued. "That means he's thinking about you."

Whatever rebukes Whisper thought about making to Chill evaporated in that last thought. In fact, Whisper was without words entirely.

"Come on," Chill prompted. "Let's go see."

The hunters approached from the same direction Whisper had seen the young man leaving, what seemed like an eternity ago. Whisper saw the young poet, his Dreamer, ahead of the other three men. He was about to rush out to him, but Chill stopped him. Instead, they observed, just as they had the other hunting parties before. Whisper was clearly anxious, but stayed hidden, to watch and listen. His Although ahead in distance from the others, judging from their appearance, Whisper guessed it was two brothers and their father, the poet seemed less ready for a hunt. The other three men carried their bows. The poet wore his over his shoulder. Reaching the trees first, the poet opened a pack, and unwrapped a cloth, revealing a plump biscuit, kept warm by the wrapping. He held the biscuit out, but did not move.

"The only thing you're going to lure with that are squirrels and other hunters," said one of the brothers, the first to catch up to him. "You're better off keeping it as a snack since you won't hit anything."

"It's not a lure," answered the poet. "It's an offering for the forest sprites."

"What?" the brother scoffed. Whisper recognized him as the brother he had seen the first day. "This isn't one of your poems or songs, Evan. We need meat for the winter. If you aren't going to focus, then give me that, I'll need the strength." The taller man snatched the biscuit from his younger brother's hands and took a bite, then shoved the rest into a pouch, stomping off into the woods. "And don't you be telling my kid these stories of yours. I want him growing up to be a proper man."

"That one is going to get such a case of shrinkage," Chill grumbled next to Whisper, but Whisper's thoughts were elsewhere.

"Evan," Whisper mused. "His name is Evan." As he said it, the young man's expression changed and he turned to look up into the trees again. The other brother and the father now reached the spot where Evan remained.

"Don't worry about him, little brother," the other said. "He's just being stubborn. Go ahead and tell your nephew your stories. They're harmless, and besides, he can't get enough of them."

"You boys go on, now," the father's voice was gruff. "Evan, get your bow ready and follow your brother. I'll be right behind you." The brothers did as they were told. When they were a ways in, the father set his bow down and opened his own pack. Rummaging through, he drew out some pieces of dried fruit and spoke to the open wood. "I'm sorry about my eldest. He takes responsibility seriously, and feels it has to come from his own effort. I know this isn't a match for Evan's offering, but I hope you'll accept it." Then he scattered the offering on the ground and followed his sons into the forest, his bow ready.

Whisper hadn't paid much attention to the other men since learning Evan's name. He did feel a light sting from the eldest brother's protest of disbelief, and a soothing of that sting came a few minutes later. But at this moment, his entire attention was on the young poet. The brothers had walked in together, and then began to fan out. Chill appeared at his side briefly.

"The father's alright, I'll let him be. Even the other brother's not bad. I'm going to get that eldest, though. I won't need to ask where you'll be. Do I?" He didn't.

As the family spread out in different directions, Whisper followed Evan. The poet seemed uneasy. Whisper noted that Evan carried his bow casually, dangling, not ready like any of the hunters had. Once he was far enough from his family, the boy started talking to himself.

"What am I doing here? I'm no hunter, but if only I could be a success at this, then just maybe…"

Evan didn't finish the thought, and Whisper wondered why it was so important to him to find success in this hunt. Then, suddenly, he realized that it didn't really matter why Evan was so desperate to succeed, it only mattered that he needed to, and more importantly, that Whisper could help.

Opening his awareness, Whisper sensed every creature in the forest. Locating a deer not far from where Evan searched, he went first to the deer, resting a hand on the back of his neck.

"My friend, I must ask a dire favor of you," he said. The deer, who had been grousing, raised his head, pressing into Whisper's hand. His ears flicked, and then he bowed his head, acknowledging the sacrifice being asked of him.

Not far away, Evan heard the wind pick up and quell down. Somehow, it seemed as if the sound had formed his name.

"No," he thought, "stay focused. If I go off daydreaming today, the teasing will never stop." He continued in the direction he'd been going before. The sound repeated, stronger this time, and somehow clearer. It wasn't speech, but somehow he could tell it was his name, as though someone out of earshot were calling him. Curiosity winning out, he turned into the direction of the voice. He wasn't sure how far he'd changed direction, or how far he'd been traveling, but he soon found himself pushing past a stand of brush, and looking directly at a calm stag, standing before him. Evan jumped slightly, then froze, worried that he would frighten the stag away. However, it was clear that the buck was already aware of him, staring back with soft black eyes.

Hesitantly, the young poet brought up his bow and reached over his shoulder to draw an arrow from its quiver, feeling a brief panic when the deer started to move. But the deer only paced in a small circle, and stopped, facing off to the side, and presenting an easy target to the would-be hunter.

"No, I can't," Evan started to say, lowering his bow, but then he heard the rustle in the wind again.

"*It's alright*," the wind seemed to say. So Evan raised the bow again, knocking and drawing back the arrow. He stood frozen for a moment. The buck dipped his head in a brief nod and turned looking directly at Evan.

"I'm so sorry," Evan said, and released the arrow. A terrible silence followed and Evan stood motionless, tears streaming down his face. Then the silence was broken by the wind returning.

"It's alright," the voice soothed. "It's alright." Evan walked up to the stag and knelt beside it.

"This isn't me," he said, laying his bow on the ground in front of the dead animal, as if in offering. "Let them ridicule me if they must, but I will no longer join them in the hunt."

When he'd recovered, Evan called for his father and brothers, who found him and set to work dressing the deer to take back. Evan's next older brother complimented him on his instincts and finding such a fine deer. The eldest simply huddled off to the side, sneezing and shivering. Completing their task, the four men carried the deer and headed home. Evan paused a moment, turning back to the woods as though he were about to say something, but then he turned back and continued on his way.

***

In the coming months, Whisper saw the father and two brothers several more times, but not Evan. Chill, of course, continued to harry the eldest brother, but Whisper no longer felt inclined toward his old games.

The fairy rings began to swell with power again, but this time there was no calling. Instead, the rings strengthened the fairies who would come into their full power on the night of Solstice.

"You know," Chill said to Whisper one evening. "On the night of the solstice, we'll be strong enough that you could leave the wood and go find him."

"I know," Whisper answered. "But if I draw on that power, I won't be able to stay here when spring comes."

"And if you remain here in spring, your choice will be made, and you'll be Summer." It was clear that Chill favored his own season, but there was also a sense that he would miss his friend if they became of different courts.

Whisper had other thoughts on his mind. He might be able to leave the forest and go see Evan on the night of Solstice, but the farther he went from the center of power, the fairy rings, the less present he would be. It was unlikely that Evan would even be aware of him. The wind hissed through the woods as Whisper debated this decision aloud in the few remaining nights before he would have to decide.

On the day of the solstice, Whisper paced the wood muttering to himself. By nightfall, he would have to decide.

"What do I do?" he yelled out to the world, hearing his voice as shaking branches. Then, he heard an echo. Not his own voice, but a voice calling his name. It was Evan's voice. The power of his Name drew Whisper to the forest's edge so quickly that it seemed like he had flown faster than any bird, passing through the trees as though they were made of mist. Suddenly, he stood at the tree he had spent his first days in, watching. It was almost unfamiliar now, the last of its leaves having fallen long ago. Whisper leaned out from the wood and could see Evan approaching, running, although Whisper couldn't tell whether Evan was running to the wood, or simply away from the village.

"Whisper!" Evan called, drawing nearing. When he reached the edge the wood, he paused to catch his breath, and then spoke again, more steadily. "Whisper, I know you're real. You led me to the deer, and even convinced it to sacrifice itself. I don't know why, but I know it was you, and right now..." his voice trailed off. "Right now I need you, because I have no one else. Not even my family."

Whisper reached out and tried to touch Evan, but Evan showed no sign of awareness that he was there. It was as if Whisper reached right through the hand as he tried to take it in his own. All Whisper could feel was despair, hurt, and loneliness. Before he could recover from the sensation, he heard Chill approaching.

"I saw you rush off like a lightning bolt, so I followed you..." he suddenly noticed Evan standing there. "...here. What is it?"

"I don't know," Whisper said. "Someone hurt him."

Anger flared in Chill, and he stormed past Whisper and Evan, passing farther beyond the wood than either he or Whisper had ever gone before. The power of Winter Solstice was rising, and Chill was quite far before he seemed to slow. Then he turned back to where Whisper stood with Evan.

"I'm going to find the brother. He is bane to us, and I intend to put his tormenting to an end."

Whisper believed him. Chill had been around for many winters, and was stronger and more experienced. Chill would not be diminished by moving away from the fairy rings as Whisper would.

The rings! Whisper realized. *If moving away from them makes it harder to be noticed…*

"Evan, follow me!" Whisper called. At first Evan just looked around in a circle, but Whisper kept moving deeper into the forest calling again and again. Though he still seemed unsure about what he was hearing, Evan started to follow in the direction where he heard the voice.

"Whisper, is that you?" Evan called.

"Yes," Whisper thought, half answering the question, and half encouraging Evan to keep using his name. He could feel it strengthening his presence, but he still felt no more substantial than mist. The woods were deep, but Whisper knew where he was going, and he continued leading Evan, who followed tirelessly.

They had traveled for hours, and as the sun set, Whisper reached the edge of the great circle where he had danced at Samhain. Evan had been following and as he ran up, he stopped just at the edge of the circle. His eyes cast about the great clearing and a look of awe and wonder crossed his face.

"This… this is… amazing," Evan breathed. Then, overcome by what he was seeing, he dropped to one knee and cast his eyes downward.

"No, Evan, don't. Please look up. Look at me!" Whisper urged, but Evan continued to look down. "You still can't see me, can you?" Whisper reached out to lift Evan's chin, but it was like reaching through him. Evan did lift his head a bit, reacting to the sensation of being touched, but when he raised his eyes, he was looking right through Whisper.

"Alright, then," Whisper declared. "Let's make this an official meeting." Whisper took a step back, making sure he was within the boundaries of the circle. He planted his feet in the ground, willing the power up into his body. He raised his arms, and streaks of light beamed toward him from the stars. The power from the earth and sky combined, giving Whisper his most substantial form yet. Finally, Whisper inhaled, drawing in the cold winter air of the longest night. The bitter air filled him and his misty form crystallized. Thousands of sensations filled Whisper as he began to really feel. None of them matched the feeling that coursed through him when his new, icy eyes, met Evan's.

"Whisper?" Evan asked. Whisper nodded. "It's really you, I'm so glad I found you. I had to find you. You helped me and no one else understands." He stood and moved toward Whisper.

"Evan, wait!" Whisper tried to warn, but it was too late. Evan's steps had taken him into the circle, and although he kept approaching, Whisper could tell that the cold was much stronger within. Most of his concern was lost, however, when the two stood face to face at last.

"What happened?" Whisper asked.

"My brother," Evan started. "I've been telling my nephew stories about you, and the other forest spirits, sharing poems I've written."

"You've written poems? About me?" Whisper felt another new sensation, blushing.

"Yes. So has my nephew, but that's the problem. My brother found a stack of the manuscripts his son wrote, and he won't let me visit anymore." Evan seemed like he wanted to say more, but he stopped there. Tears fell from his eyes, and Whisper reached up to brush them away. Evan flinched at the coldness of the touch, but didn't withdraw.

"Don't worry. You'll be able to see your nephew again, and your brother won't hurt you anymore." Whisper sounded so gentle and assuring with this news.

"What do you mean?" asked Evan.

"When I saw that you were hurt, I knew it was your brother. My friend, Chill, is a powerful member of the Winter Court, and tonight is the Winter Solstice. He has gone to put an end to your brother's cruelty."

"No!" cried Evan. "Please call him back. My brother doesn't understand, but he doesn't mean to hurt. Please stop your friend." Whisper didn't agree, but the look of terror in Evan's eyes told him something was wrong. He willed his thoughts to take him to the edge of the forest… and nothing happened.

"I can't," Whisper admitted. "In this form, I can't move as fast anymore." At this news, Evan turned and started running. Whisper ran after him, catching him by the arm. "Wait! There's nothing we can do now. It's probably already too late!" Whisper watched Evan's face taking in the news, neither of them even noticing that Evan's arm had gone limp where Whisper still gripped it. Suddenly, Evan threw his other arm around Whisper, embracing him.

"This is all my fault. I never should have come here." Evan began sobbing.

"I'm glad you came," Whisper returned the embrace with both arms, feeling the fading warmth of his Dreamer. "It'll be alright. You can raise your nephew, now, and no one will ever hurt you again." For a moment, Whisper thought that Evan was trying to control his sobbing, but when he released his hold enough to step back, he realized that Evan was struggling to breathe.

"Oh no, Evan!" he cried. Ice crystals cracked in the higher branches from his cry. "Hold on, I'll get you home." But as Whisper took Evan in his arms to carry him, he realized that it was his touch that was freezing him. He set Evan down and stood, thinking to call on the animals to help him.

"It's alright," he heard Evan say, his voice very weak. "I don't

105

want to go back. I couldn't face my nephew knowing I'm the reason his father is dead. I don't think I can make it anyway. Please just hold me again. Let my last moments be with you."

Whisper wanted to fight, he wanted to fade back into mist again so that he could leave, or get help, or do something. But he knew he could not leave Evan for even a moment. And he also knew that there was nothing he can do anymore. Kneeling down, he took Evan into his arms, held him close, and wept.

Whisper wasn't sure how long he'd been holding Evan, nor how long ago Evan had stopped breathing. It didn't matter. He continued to hold the body of the poet who gave him life, and nothing would turn his thoughts from his vigil. Nothing that is, except for the radiance of powerful and majestic presence behind him. The presence was unmistakable. Hesitantly, but unable to do otherwise, Whisper stood and turned to face the Winter Queen.

"Whisper, is that your name?" the queen asked. Her voice felt even colder than Chill's. Whisper only nodded, then lowered into a bow. "Rise, Whisper. I have been watching you since Samhain. You are quite remarkable. You inspired a dreamer to write about us winter fairies."

"Yes, your majesty, but I'm afraid I also.." Whisper started to confess, but realized it wasn't necessary.

"I know. It had to be I suppose. The winter court must always be the ones handling the unpleasant necessities. You helped this poet give his family what they wanted of him, but they rejected the gift that he was meant to bring them. They can only realize his value by losing him. Perhaps they will be appreciative of the next generation."

"I doubt the nephew will be inspired to write poems about us when he's lost his father," Whisper mused, then added "and his uncle."

"He still has a father," Chill's voice broke into the conversation. A moment later, Chill himself approached, pausing to offer a deep bow to the queen. "I'm sorry, Whisper. I couldn't do it. When I found the home, the eldest was lecturing his son about wasting time on such fantasies, but agreed to listen to one of the boy's poems. It was good… really good. The eldest said so too, and he promised to apologize to Evan as soon as he got back."

"It's too late now," Whisper said sullenly.

"Indeed," said the queen, "and for you, Whisper, there is no turning back. You have drawn on the power of winter are part of my court now."

"Of course my queen," Whisper replied. "I will serve you well."

In the days that followed, a few search parties came to the forest, attempting to find the lost Evan. They were met with the coldest of temperatures, and haunting voices in the wood. They left with only the knowledge that the forest was angry. That anger remains for many today. It can be felt in the cold air and heard in the hissing wind. Over the years, some have even perished in the wood, their bodies found just within its borders. But the body of a young poet was never found.

For at the spring gathering, as the summer court took their place again, Whisper went to the site where Evan breathed last. The body had remained timeless, Evan's wish to spend his last moments with Whisper still showing in a serene expression. As the great dance ended, Whisper carried the body of his one love, and his first victim, into the dreaming.

Marcus Maichle

Marcus Maichle *has been making up stories since grade school. He currently lives in the Milwaukee area, and looks forward to being able to tell stories to his niece, Amanda.*

Ambush

Mark Scheef

Ambush

One

My eyes struggled to find focus and I spent a moment shaking
away the confusion of waking somewhere other than my own bed.
My hands and backside registered pain from the cold and something in
the back of my mind wondered when I stopped noticing the same pain
in my feet. I woke up half-sitting, half-squatting in a shallow hole in
the ground surrounded by pine trees and patches of night sky.

I was in a foxhole far from home and I was supposed to be
watching for Germans.

Crap.

Eyes darting left and right, I swallowed hard wondering if
something had awakened me. Where the stars reached in through the
canopy, columns of light illuminated ice crystals forming on the wet
pine needles. Where it couldn't reach it left dark shadows to play
across my mind.

After a few moments without spotting any movement my
adrenaline died down and left room for a little logic to fight its way
back to the surface. Our squad was miles away from the enemy line -
which hadn't moved in months. The only reason they left me out at
this Observation Point alone was because there was nothing to
observe.

... well, that and I was the new guy who had just shipped in.

... and the rest of the squad was having a grand time celebrating back
in the little village without me.

My M1 rifle sat in the dirt at the bottom of the foxhole exactly where it shouldn't be and I reached down to put it back on my lap. It was the closest thing you could get to a security blanket out here.

"Nap time over Junior?" came a voice standing right above and behind me.

I nearly leaped into the air. Instead, since I was already in the process of leaning over, I launched myself into the side of my poorly dug foxhole and lay twisted at the bottom looking up at Adams.

"Holy ..." was about all I got out as my first recognizable sentence, "You ... you scared the crap out of me."

The stupid grin on his face might have irritated me if it wasn't for the dread fear and awe I held for each and every one of my squad. These guys had spent months fighting and killing Germans to get to this little spot somewhere in Belgium. They had run straight into enemy machine gun nests, mortar fire and minefields just to kill more Germans. Not all of them made it, but the ones still here were forged from something stronger than me.

I just got to this war. A late recruit. I had never killed anything.

When the Japanese bombed Pearl Harbor, every young man in the nation signed up to fight. Not me...at least not at first. It took a convincing speech from my father before I followed along and was thankfully assigned to an army desk job. I think it was obvious even then I wasn't fighting material. If I hadn't fallen asleep at that same desk at the wrong time I would still be warm and dry right now and not scared out of my mind.

I sat up and did my best to recover some pride. With a flourish I gestured to the edge of the foxhole, "may I offer you a seat?" Adams flopped down on the ground and when he leaned over I smelled alcohol on his breath.

Ambush

"Did you know there was a winery down in that valley?"

Of course I did. It was the reason the new guy was the only one volunteered to spend the night in a muddy foxhole.

"And the Belgians were happy to share a little?" I ventured. This was already more conversation than I'd had with the entire squad.

"Oh yes. Very much so," he pointed to his cheek where I could see the faint smudge of lipstick, "and more than one little beauty has shown her appreciation to the American rescuers."

I smiled with him. These guys hadn't seen a moment of respite since they fought their way onto occupied French shores. I tried to set my own complaints aside - they deserved any break they could catch.

Adams pulled off his helmet and pointed to the side. On it was etched a four-leaf clover, the unofficial symbol of our unit. No soldier could etch their own, it only came from proving yourself to the group. My smile vanished as I remembered the distance in experiences between us. That symbol meant something to each and every member of the unit and I was the only one who didn't wear it.

With an uncoordinated slap to the back of my head, Adams knocked my helmet off and the two sat next to each other in stark contrast. What had I ever done, and I mean ever, to earn something like that.

Through an expression I couldn't read, Adams looked down at the helmets, "Junior, this has been the best day since we landed on this hell. Trust me when I say you are missing out on one of the great moments of history in that little village." Pulling out his bayonet, he started scratching the four-leaf symbol on my still-smooth helmet.

I looked up at him in disbelief, "What are you doing?"

"For unquestion... unquestioninging ... For *extraordinary* personal sacrifice in the face of..." he paused looking up, "almost certain drunken bliss and jubilation, you are now a member of the Lucky Losers." It was not the prettiest four ... wait... five-leaf clover I had ever seen, but it was done. He placed the helmet back on my head and from somewhere a bottle of wine showed up in his hand. Without a word, he stood up and stumbled back down the valley.

I had surprisingly mixed feelings about my new award as it was only through dumb luck that I had just received it. While I doubted I would ever really deserve it, part of me would be happy if I never needed to.

Two

Double crap.

I had fallen asleep in my foxhole again. I didn't mean to - in fact I had taken two quick walks since Adams left just to get blood moving back to my feet again. I heard whispering ahead of me and guessed Adams or someone else was trying to put the scare in me again. With a smirk I lifted my head ... and froze.

Silhouetted by a small flashlight was a circle of soldiers huddled around someone with an unfolded map. The light leaking from between the soldiers lit the distinctive rims of their helmets ... German helmets.

For a brief moment I prayed I was dreaming. Was I seriously looking at ... I needed to count ... eight Germans no more than forty feet in front of me? I slowly glanced down again to see my rifle stowed underneath my legs. How in the world did that get ... never mind. Did I really think for even a moment I could take on eight Germans? I looked up to see the circle split open toward me. Light spilled up onto the face holding the map and sculpted his features into an almost demonic relief. Without looking down he pointed through me, right to my soul.

I screamed.

Luckily I was still too scared to *actually* scream. But trust me that on the inside I was really busy with it. It turns out he wasn't a demon and he wasn't pointing at my soul. But he was still just as terrifying; he was pointing the way to the winery and my squad.

To my own credit, a tiny part of me started calculating the odds of unclipping a grenade and digging my rifle out of the dirt before getting shot. The circle of Germans stood up and so did two new shapes right next to my foxhole. I mean right. next. to. my. foxhole. I actually gasped and swung my head fast enough for my helmet buckles to smack into my face. Fortunately, any noise I made was lost in the creaking of gear the soldiers were shouldering. I could see a deadly belt-fed machine gun hanging from one of them and the matching tripod strapped to his buddy. Considering how fast those could spit out bullets once they were set up, I was sure more soldiers were around to help carry the thousands of rounds intended for us. As the circle broke up, I confirmed my guess as more shapes moved through the trees toward the village ... I was a single unprepared soldier surrounded by a full platoon of Germans.

I had no idea how they passed by without spotting me. I just sat as still as possible staring at my knees and inventing new prayers. As soon as the last footsteps were behind me, I decided to retreat away from the village with the idea that I might be able to find some kind of help. It started well enough with me quietly grabbing my rifle and getting up into a crouch. It was when I crawled out of the hole, caught my rifle on the edge and listened to it clatter back to the bottom that I just took off without it ... running away.

Right into more Germans.

Maybe if I hadn't been so busy looking behind me I wouldn't have aimed myself directly into possibly the only other two enemies out there. One was a smaller man crouched over a radio while the other was the size of a small tank, with a rifle ready in his hands. I skidded to a stop and there was a moment of prolonged stillness between the three of us. Only a blur of motion later, however, and the big man's rifle was pointed at my skull. The smaller man waved his hands, "Wolf, Nein! Nein!" Wolf? Really? Couldn't I have run into someone named Mouse? Or maybe Bambi?

I slowly put my hands in the air to prove I wasn't any kind of threat. The big guy moved a few steps closer and I had to look up to see him towering over me. Now I realized why I had thought the radio man was small. This Wolf guy eclipsed normal people. Personally, I would have named him something larger like "Bull" or even "Moose" if it wasn't for the fact that his presence made me feel like a lone deer caught in the open. A predatory grin crept over his face and the butt of his rifle landed hard on the side of my head.

Mark Scheef

Ambush

Three

This time I didn't open my eyes so gently. While I may have been groggily waking back up on my own, being dropped onto the cold ground finished the job much more efficiently. I was lying on my back looking up at the night sky through a low-hanging spiral of pine branches. It should have been peaceful really. I could have even napped here for a while if it wasn't for my throbbing head and something that kept bumping my leg.

I rocked my head just a bit to see what was happening and cleared the last of the hazy confusion from my thoughts. Some kind of cloth gag was wrapped between my teeth and tied behind my head. My involuntary nap had given my eyes plenty of time to adjust to the dim light. A rucksack sat by my legs and the Wolf squatted next to me digging through it. I could make out my own hands tied in front of me, but I couldn't see if my feet were in the same shape without moving and alerting my captor.

The Wolf let out a soft grunt of victory and pulled a length of rope from the bag. Stretching his arms to straighten out the tangles, he looked up to a knot caught in his raised hand. If I had given my next action any thought at all, I'm pretty sure I would have politely sat still and let the brute carry me off as a prisoner of war. I'm almost certain I wouldn't have done anything dumb enough to provoke him.

Since the opportunity was so sudden, however, I skipped the thinking step. As soon as he looked up, I rolled both knees up against my chest. Glimpsing my movement, he looked down just as I kicked out with everything I had in me. He managed to deflect one foot with his arm, but fortunately my feet were not yet tied together and I managed to tag the toe of my boot across his nose. With a speed that belied his size, he launched himself onto his own feet to escape a second blow ... but straight into the web of pine boughs hanging above him.

While I don't really speak any German, it didn't take much to interpret the string of curses growled out as he smashed the offending branches. I rolled away from the tree until I could stand up. Once on my feet, I ran low with my arms in front of my face to avoid getting my eyes gouged by unforgiving brush and barreled blindly through the forest. I was certain I could hear my pursuer on my trail and pushed my legs harder, ripping the gag from my mouth to breathe cool air and get up to full speed. I had no idea where I was, but I knew I was a fast runner and my smaller frame could cover ground longer than the big bad Wolf. When my legs and lungs finally did give up the sprint, I still kept up a jog. I looked back as often as I could, but saw no movement in the brush behind me.

Coming up to a grass clearing glowing under the stars, I fell to my knees and tried to calm my breath to something quieter than a series of gasps. I began to notice a distant yelling out past the open area ahead of me. Still breathing hard enough to make me nauseous, I crept forward into the opening and found myself looking down our shallow valley and the moonlit winery it contained. A blazing bonfire burned near the cluster of buildings framed by a white stone wall that skirted the property. I stopped to listen again and realized the yelling I had heard was actually singing. I could see my squad and the locals dancing, drinking, and definitely singing around the fire far below.

They had no idea their performance was drawing an audience determined to kill them.

Four

Once again I acted without thinking. I waved my bound arms and yelled to my distant squad. The volume of my voice surprised me as it carried across the night air. The dancers didn't pause, the singers never faltered. Despite my antics, I couldn't get the attention of anyone at the bonfire.

I did, however, get a reaction from others down in the valley. Behind the stone wall outside the winery, a series of dim flashing signal lights erupted. Matching lights came from the edge of the surrounding woods followed by shadows moving toward the stone wall. The Germans had made their way into the valley and were preparing to wipe out my unsuspecting squad. If they had known how few of our soldiers were actually down there, they might have already opened fire.

I couldn't really stop a platoon of Germans, but maybe I could warn my team. I had no idea how I would accomplish it just yet, but first things first: I had to get my hands untied.

A little ways along the hill crest I could see the grey stones of an old building glowing in the moonlight and once again I was off running. This time my night-adjusted eyes had an open field without shadows and I covered the distance without having to fear each step. Before I could reach what looked to be a barn I rolled over a wooden fence and tested my wrist bindings against it. Not quite sharp enough, I needed something like ... I looked around ... like the stone corner of the barn itself.

I was back to gasping by the time I pressed my bonds against the sharp stone corner and I pumped my legs up and down to get a cutting motion without tearing my own wrists. As the stone tore through the last of the fibrous rope, I chuckled to myself and wondered what my assault on this barn corner might look like to any random Belgian who happened to stroll by.

My humor was a bit short lived.

Cold metal pressed against my throat, freezing me in place and I remembered it wasn't embarrassment from the locals that would kill me out here. I already guessed who my assailant was even before huge hands spun me around to face his ridiculously broad chest. I looked up and was a little surprised and a little cheered to see an unnatural bend to the Wolf's bloodied nose. At least I knew he could be hurt and it reminded me that I hadn't lost just yet.

Holding me against the wall, he slipped the knife back into his belt and wound his free hand back to put his full weight behind a punch. I'm sure it was intended to drop me into unconsciousness for the fourth time tonight, but I wouldn't let this one be so easy. As his right fist came down I slammed my head forward into the punch, letting it connect with the top of my helmet.

Somehow I thought I would barely notice when the helmet absorbed the blow. Instead, a painfully loud bell was dropped somewhere inside my skull and my neck and spine each felt two inches shorter. I was stunned and stumbling, but I heard two things that kept me in the fight. The first was the sound of something besides me cracking when the Wolf's punch landed and the second was a howl of pain and anger from the nearly indomitable Wolf.

As soon as I found my feet I plowed low into the surprised Wolf with everything I had. I could feel his feet leave the ground enough to kick him off balance, but even then he managed to twist before we fell leaving me to hit the ground hard and sending us both rolling down the inclined field.

We turned over more than a few times before I found myself pinned to the ground with the Wolf straddled across my stomach. He was protecting his smashed right hand at his side, but his left still managed to connect a solid blow to my ribs and then to my head. I actually tried to roll my head into the punch again before realizing both of our helmets had come off in the fall. His fist left a gash on my forehead pouring blood and stars into my vision. Even though I had finally managed to free my hands from the rest of the loosened rope, they merely fell limply to the side as I did my best to hold onto consciousness.

After my dumb forehead-to-fist maneuver, the Wolf actually laughed at me. I could plainly see his feral grin in the dim light as he reached down and pulled the knife back out with his good hand. I didn't feel like dying in the first place, but there no way I was going down without some kind of fight. Laying on my back without any advantage in size or strength I had to think through dizziness and pain and think fast. My outstretched hand fell onto something familiar and I gave the Wolf a smile of my own.

Fingers closed around the edge of my fallen helmet and I swung it hard at his right side, letting the Wolf's own fighting instincts take over. He reached out with his broken hand to block the blow and actually yelped when it connected. The helmet bounced straight back so I swung again as the Wolf shuffled backward in surprise. He leaned forward to get his feet underneath him and my third swing connected dead center in his face. Blood flowed freely from his nose and I grabbed hold of his uniform to follow him down as he toppled backward.

From on top of his chest I swung my helmet into his face again and the knife fell from his grasp.

I swung again. I had never asked him to fight me.

Another blow to his face. I never wanted to be in this war.

And another. I just wanted to make it home alive.

And another ... again ... and again. I was willing to do whatever I needed to get there.

The Wolf had long stopped moving and I looked away from the smashed face, staring instead at the wet dents in my helmet. Somehow the engraved five-leaf clover had survived and by some means I had shared a bit of that luck.

The Lucky Losers. Adams. My squad. I'd need just a bit more of that luck if they were to survive as well in the next few minutes. I looked back up at the barn and at the shadowy object I could now see inside.

Ambush

Five

With a final shove the old truck rolled out of the barn to the edge of the sloped field. I hauled myself up to the driver's seat as soon as the momentum pulled faster than my legs could keep up. The relic had been sitting in the barn with its engine completely missing and the back filled to the top with cut firewood, but I counted four wheels and a steering bar which was all I needed to make good time down the hill.

From here the moon lit the downhill terrain between me and the stone wall where the German signal lights had flashed. There were a few strips of trees I could avoid and a rather long dip where I would approach without being seen. My plan was to roll this massive truck down to the edge of that last hillcrest where I would tie off the steering bar and send it crashing down into the midst of the Germans. If this didn't catch the attention of my drunken squad, nothing would.

The plan sounded great at first, but once I started rolling I realized I hadn't factored everything into it. The field leading down to the winery wasn't quite as smooth as it first looked in the dark and I found myself nearly bucked out of my seat before I could determine where the brakes were. Chunks of bouncing firewood rained down around me into the roofless cab as I pushed at every pedal without effect. In mere moments I was hurtling at a velocity never envisioned by the original designer. By the time I dropped into the hidden dip, the seat had broken away and was bouncing around the cab along with the firewood and I was crouched like a horse jockey doing everything I could to keep from becoming airborne.

I had really imagined the scenario as keeping just barely enough momentum to carry me to the edge of the last hilltop, but instead I was barely holding onto a rocket learning to fly. I forced myself to look down at my controls one more time and found two long handles that had been somewhat hidden by the edge of the former seat. I reached down, grabbed them both in one hand, and pulled hard.

As if turning off a switch, everything went still. Utter confusion raced ahead of any explanations my mind could come up with until I looked back up. For what seemed like an eternity I could see the horizon rise over the bumper, followed by the winery's bonfire, and the rapidly approaching stone wall. In reality, only a second or two had passed since the truck leaped off the top of the last hillcrest and time sped back to normal with a landing hard enough to send my chest into the steering bar and knock the wind out of me.

Despite the shock and screaming pain in my chest, I kept a death grip on the steering bar until I was bounced back upright again. Immediately I could see the truck was on a beeline run to the Germans. They had formed a pile of stones up the side of the wall and I could even see the silhouette of their oversized machine gun being handed up to the top. All the darting shadows at the wall stopped moving to stare at the rolling juggernaut spitting dirt and logs and I realized this was my cue to make an exit. I hadn't really wanted to leap off a moving truck, but the alternative of crashing into a thick stone wall had to be worse. I let go and jumped.

Or more accurately, I fell halfway out of the truck. Somehow my boot caught on the broken seat frame and I hung partway out the side watching my death fast approach. Reaching back up to the steering bar, I pulled hard to turn the truck away from the wall. The wheels managed only a slight change of course before the speed and pressure of the turn snapped their spokes. The front corner of the truck buried into the dirt flipping it upside down and turning its forward motion into an airborne roll.

What happened next can only be described as surreal – as if time itself was savoring what could be my last moments on earth. I was floating and spinning high through the air. On the far side of the wall I could now see the happy celebration with Adams and the rest dancing by the fire. Below me a sluggish wall of firewood had launched itself toward the piled stones and into the group of Germans frozen in surprise. Somewhere behind that the truck was tumbling forward - but too slowly to be real. In fact, until I struck the ground again, I had been sure I was dead – merely a ghost passing on.

Maybe this was why I wasn't too concerned at first about bouncing and skidding into the middle of some really unhappy German soldiers.

Mark Scheef

Ambush

Six

I wasn't actually dead just yet, but it felt close enough. I gave up trying to pinpoint which part of my body ached most and did my best to sit up instead. Dust from my crash hung in the night air, but I could see around me well enough to get my bearings. I had landed at the base of the wall next to the stones piled by the Germans. Most of the enemy soldiers had been somewhere to the left of the stone pile while the truck and most of its deadly cargo had tumbled to the right of it. It wasn't exactly a pretty scene to the right, but I could be fairly certain the soldiers on that side were not going to be doing any more fighting.

Back to the left I could hear confused Germans and see shapes pointing their guns into the dark looking for what enemy force had spoiled their surprise. Not wanting to stick around when they found out, I tried to crawl back around to the right of the stone pile only to find a hand holding me down. I was laying on top of a German soldier who must have taken the brunt of my landing for me. He was holding on to my jacket with one hand and reaching out to his fallen rifle with the other. He yelled something to his companions and at the edge of my vision I could see a number of them moving toward us. I had to get out of the situation fast. I lifted my body to wind up a punch with whatever I had left in me and stopped short. Strapped across the front of this guy was an entire explosives depot - six potato masher grenades hung from a bandolier on his chest. I still threw a quick punch toward his face, but only to force him to pull his hand up and off my jacket. With my other hand I reached down, yanked the cap and ball fuse off one of the grenades and dove over the rocks.

I guess the delay on a grenade can seem like a long time when people are trying to kill you. At about two seconds I could hear soldiers running up to their injured comrade. At about three I heard what were probably instructions to find me. Four seconds and I had already been spotted behind the rocks and there was even more yelling back to the others. If the grenade had given them even a half-second more, I would have faced a firing squad of revenge. Instead, when the combination of grenades went off it seared my vision and sent rocks splintering into the wall behind me. The soldier who spotted me was not nearly as lucky and I guessed a few more behind him were in the same situation.

Dust plumed from the explosion and my ears registered only a high pitched buzz. Desperate for some type of sensory awareness, I felt around and found someone lying next to me where there had been only stones a moment before. Since the body didn't move at my touch, I reached out further for anything useful and found its hand wrapped around an unfamiliar German rifle. My ears gained back a few tones and I could hear heavy gunfire coming from fairly close by. Swirls of dust by my head told me the passage of bullets was only inches from my head. I scrambled to pry the hand from the gun and dragged it into my arms. It seemed a lot bigger and heavier than I expected, but I was not about to argue a few pounds when I was mere moments from being riddled with bullets.

I got my feet under me in order to heft the gun to my hip. Since I couldn't really see my opponents, I pointed the dangerous end somewhere toward the incoming fire and pulled the trigger. Staccato flashes of light and a stream of glowing-red tracer bullets spewed from the barrel and arced into the sky as I fell flat on my back from the recoil. This wasn't just some really heavy rifle, this was the true machine gun I had seen the German soldiers carrying in to destroy my squad. It was never meant to be fired without its tripod or at least a bipod, but it was all I had for now. I rolled back to my feet and was getting a better grip on the machine gun when two Germans stepped through the last of the cloud with their rifles pointed my direction.

I never had a chance to really aim but I did manage to fire first. The bright flashes of gunfire highlighted the wide eyes of the German soldiers. They skidded, turned and ran without one of the wild shots ever touching them. Not believing I could have missed, I fired another spray of bullets from the bulky gun and ran after them. As soon as I cleared the cloud of dust I found the first line of Germans fleeing into a second line of Germans. I fought back my own urge to escape and pulled the trigger again. The long belt of ammunition flailed behind me, snaking up into the gun yanking it left and right while the recoil launched the gun skyward. I couldn't really keep the gun under control and the glowing fire sprayed out into the ground and across the sky around them. Facing a curtain of red tracers and nowhere to hide, the second line broke and followed the first toward the far treeline with me on their heels.

I chased the platoon into the trees before I realized I was screaming some kind of war cry. The sound of my own voice surprised me and I looked around to see that the machine gun had stopped booming. My fingers were burning on the shroud surrounding the glowing barrel and the ammunition belt that had been trailing me was now nothing but a path of empty brass casings on the ground. It took me a moment for the reality of my situation to come back to me. I was standing alone with an empty gun in an open field halfway between the wall and the treeline - the treeline where half a platoon of enemy soldiers were now regrouping.

Like popcorn reaching critical temperature, the silence was broken by first one shot and then a couple more until the edge of the woods erupted with muzzle flashes. For a moment I stood in shock listening to bullets buzz past me before remembering the difference between 'brave' and 'stupid' was whether you survived to tell the tale. I dropped the gun and ran back toward the wall. I had made it only a few steps before something tore through my thigh and sent me sprawling. I couldn't believe I had made it even this far, but I was still mad as hell that with hundreds of rounds and a surplus of targets I had not managed to hit a single thing, yet with their first few shots I was already taken down. Fueled by frustration, I used my rolling momentum to push back onto my good leg until I could limp toward the wall again. My goal was to use the stone pile to climb over to where I hoped my squad was sober enough not to shoot me before I got to them and explained what was happening.

The shots behind me trickled to a slow sputter and I looked over my shoulder to see every last German I had chased away from the wall now performing the reverse - and gaining quickly. With pain still racing through my leg, I increased my faltering pace to something more like a flailing skip and set my focus on the wall. In fact, if I hadn't been so focused on it I might not have seen Adam's head and hand poking over the top waving at me and signaling me to keep running to the right. I was only ten steps from avoiding a charging horde of angry Germans and Adams wanted me to instead keep running out in the open. I thought long and hard about it - at least five whole steps - before I followed orders and turned to the right.

I looked over my shoulder and was surprised to see that the closest Germans had been only 20 feet behind me. The first two stepped out of the way while the rest charged at the stone ramp leading up the wall. My leg gave out while I was twisted around and I bounced to the ground with even more pain shooting through my leg. I was watching the two lead Germans aim their rifles where I lay when I saw the first volley of grenades fly over the wall from the other side and into the middle of them. Someone yelled what sounded a foreign version of "Grenade" and I threw my own face down into the dirt. Explosions detonated too close for comfort and I started belly-crawling toward the rolled truck for cover. A second series of explosions followed the first knocking me flat again. This time I was too tired to crawl any further and laid very still as the gunshots behind me faded away.

Seven

When I opened my eyes again I was staring into a painfully bright light.

"Junior, you in there? You awake?" came a voice from behind the light.

"Depends on who's asking," I replied, "if you're a German then I might be more polite about where I tell you to stick that thing."

The light disappeared with a click and I could see the serious face of Private James, our squad's medic, hovering above me. With a glance he looked up to the rest of the squad standing around me, "Yeah, I think he'll be just fine, just check that he remembers his name every hour tonight - looks like something big knocked him square in the back of the head."

"I told you we threw those grenades too soon," came a reply from Adams, "Why couldn't we have let Junior climb to safety first?" From the ground I could see him standing behind my head, still swaying from too much wine.

Someone else added, "I can't believe we almost killed one of our own." Around the circle I could see a few others nodding in agreement. Our Sergeant looked up at all of them and the nodding stopped.

I interrupted the minor mutiny with my own comment, "No, you did it right. I pretty much screwed up everything I touched tonight. If you had waited another second, I would have been dead." I sat up to see everyone and tried not to grimace from the pain, "You saved my life tonight."

Maybe I was still mumbling incoherently from the concussion because there was a long moment of quiet after I spoke. Sarge broke it with his voice that never mumbled, "Did you hear that? We saved *his* life tonight." A couple chuckles came from the squad as he continued, "Junior, I think we can trust you to keep us safe for the rest of the night. Pick the most sober men to watch shifts and make sure they check in with you every hour. Give me a full report in the morning when we're sober."

"Yessir," I stammered.

Addressing the rest of the squad he added, "and would someone besides Adams fix that damn clover on his helmet?"

Ambush

Born in Wisconsin on the shores of Lake Michigan,
Mark Scheef *suffered a difficult childhood of caring parents, friendly Midwest neighbors, and quality education. This recipe for disaster was even further aggravated by good careers, supportive friends, and an incredible wife.*

Trapped in this upward spiral, he desperately sought to express elements missing from his life and, regrettably, turned to writing. Although finally able to express pain, hardship and sorrow, it was not without a terrible price. Somehow, despite his best efforts, his writing has made him happier than ever.

Mark now gets by in a sunny, warm desert in the Southwest where he is hiking in beautiful mountains, flying airplanes, and interviewing others lucky enough to have unpleasant experiences worth immortalizing in words.

My Life In Drool

Catalino Tolejano, II

My Life In Drool

I feel so loathsome.

I'm sitting on a bench in a pedestrian walkway. There's a light mist of fall rain lightly coating me and the world in a cleansing layer of water. It's cold and damp, which I only get academically as I've become less and less sensitive to the varying temperatures. That's probably why I haven't started wearing the right clothes for the season. I'll have to remember that tomorrow, to unpack the cool-weather clothes. I'm feeling lethargic in the cool weather, though, a definite sign of my condition progressing.

A couple strolls by, keeping their distance and its surprising that I didn't notice them sooner. Their pace quickens slightly and I can taste the stink of fear from both and the raw hormones on him. She's drunk, but also suffering from something making her nearly incoherent, like Rohypnol it seems. Perhaps he can feel my glare? He ushers her a little quicker as they stumble down the street away from me. He does his halfhearted best to keep her from being pummeled as the misting rain evolves into a true downpour, but it only seems for appearance sake. Perhaps it's my clothing that scared them? Shorts and a t-shirt in forty-five degree weather in the rain probably doesn't sit well with the normals. Or maybe it's because I'm sitting on this park bench, next to the sidewalk, not twenty feet from a covered bus-stop bench - at eleven in the evening, wide-eyed, glaring, and unhurried in the pouring rain? Probably looks like I'm strung out on something bad. That's what I would think. I should move before some Samaritan tries to help me. Or call the cops. I wonder if I can catch pneumonia still?

I stand up, sliding my feet into the flip-flops under the bench. The cold water has pooled in them yet it is barely tingling the soles and toes of my feet as it is forced out. God I wish I could feel even that again. Just to feel the little sensations of everyday life again. I'd be happy to give up the ability to smell almost every creature for fifty feet. Admittedly, being able to tell where they are and where they're going makes me feel pretty cool. The smells, even in the rain, merge into a bitter-sweet mix; like the alluring aroma around a restaurant but saturated with a pungent-decay odor from nearby trash bins.

As I start moving, a car rushes past then makes a u-turn blinding me with its headlights. The sensation is almost unbearable, but at least I feel something. I'm learning to get better with the blindness in the lights - I don't want to be the idiot wearing sunglasses at night and on a rainy evening. My 'normal' sight has weakened significantly: I am mostly blind during the day, with an acute sensitivity to the bright ambient light. But at night? Oh, at night I'm able to see better than I ever did during the day! Possibly better than other nocturnal creatures. I still even see colors at night, and to some degree heat emanating in the darkness. It's hard to explain, but warmth and colors stand out so distinctly, it's like the night has its own sun shining on all the dark corners of the world for me alone to see. Problem is, most people are less active at night – so what the hell am I supposed to see?

I head toward Roe street, where it's quiet, with more street lights off than on – gotta love city efficiency. I've become pretty efficient too! Well, I've become a lot of things. Many not so good, but some extraordinary. When the doctors couldn't help, I had to – no, I was driven to- find out for myself what was happening to me. I've spent months now, sitting in libraries across the nation, savoring the clean smells of the papers and the prey found there. I've been studying and learning about myself. Learning about what all the bad dreams and the terrors and the cold and the dark and the strange cravings have all meant. I was never an academic, nor even interested in books much. But now I know. At least, I feel like this is right. I'm not a vampire, which I had been thinking before I figured things out. I'm not a werewolf. I'm not a zombie – well, unless I'm playing a video game or watching football. I'm not some crazed lunatic thinking he's an elf or an extraterrestrial trapped on Earth, either. I have a real condition, but no one seemed to know what it is. No, I'm many things. But most clearly – I'm a ghoul.

My Life In Drool

***

I wasn't always like this...

I can't say for sure when I started to change. I have no event like being bitten by a wolf nor chewed on by zombies to explain my condition. What I can say is that I start dating the symptoms back over more than a year. And what a terrible, and exciting, year it has been!

I got sick with the flu. And no, I didn't work for some government or private agency working on super-secret viruses or something when I got sick. I had the flu. My wife insisted that I had pneumonia and basically delivered me to the nearest clinic once I was too sick to effectively keep her from stuffing me in the car. They cleared it up, but when I went back for follow-up I was having a few new and erratic symptoms not consistent with nor following pneumonia. I became tired often, I had some strange sensations in my chest, trouble breathing and being out of breath, and I collapsed from vertigo or something a few times. The first time I figured was just a fluke. The second fall scared the crap out of the kids and me something fierce. Eventually, they referred me to a Cardiologist who ended up with the prognosis of something called "AFib" or Atrial Fibrillation. Basically, it's an irregular heartbeat or Arrhythmia. Sounded like it made sense, so we started looking into lifestyle changes for me. Ever notice they always start with diet and exercise, the lemmings. We considered medications too, of course, but decided against that course since my (reported) symptoms were far and few between.

As the lifestyle changes did enough to keep me from further falls, in spite of increased additional symptoms, I started to get back to full work days. I had been benched behind a desk on the two construction sites I was managing, which allowed me to get to any appointments and handle things with the kids until Summer. Summer was, theoretically, when they could be home alone. Problem is, the kids could be home, but not quite home alone *together*. When Summer did hit, my wife's parents and extended family took over with the kids,

143

thank God. It's nice to know that they're surrounded by family, even if I'm not there. And believe me, it's better for us all that I'm not.

***

I stagger down Roe street, a little from my sensory overload but more to play the part of a potential victim to the other predators of the night. It isn't quite as dark as I had hoped. There's intermittent flashes from the street lights creating a kaleidoscope visual effect for me, and the jackhammer of rain on my ears is thankfully softened by my earplugs. I can see the water cleansing the dark alleys of a myriad of offensive smells - from rotten beer to urine-soaked vomit. It takes a lot of control to keep my mind focused with all the distracting sensations. I think about the cold I *should* feel and how a normal person would react to the weather, but I can't really mimic it well. I probably look like a strung-out fishing lure wriggling its way through rain. Maybe this is why I still haven't been successful in finding my first prey.

What's this?! The man standing under the darkened street lamp ahead is eying me with erratic determination! At about twenty feet I can see and smell several things that make me yearn for him to be the thug he appears - wood, metal, dirty oil, tobacco, butane, and plenty of body odor – yes, even in the rain with this guy! The bulges under his overcoat, hair and water cascading from his wide-brimmed hat in the rain, unshaven face still clutching the food of what could be his last meal, and even the nervous look in his eye all indicate the kind of scavenger I've been trying to attract! It looks like walking dark roads in less-than-hospitable parts of the city might finally pay off! The scene is perfectly set in rain, darkness, and cold. I've worked hard to keep my conscience happy. Tonight, I will finally find out if my craving is just the yearning of a crazy person or something actually physiological for me. No one will miss *this* guy, right? That's what I tell myself as I approach, putting myself between him and the pitch-black alley. The perfect opportunity and bait. Now I just need him to strike.

***

My Life In Drool

"Jesus, what a waste of my frigging' time..." I rambled on all the way to my apartment building. "Do I look like I smoke?" Needless to say I'm over the edge now and teetering on chaos as my encounter with the 'thug' hadn't gone well. "A damned sales pitch for Pot. Sonuva! Grrrr..." and the colorful expletives continue. I probably look like a madman arguing with himself out-loud as he wanders down the street, soaking wet and oblivious to everything.

As karma dictates, the rain diminished into only a slight nuisance by the time I reach my apartment building where I've got a decent corner loft on the 6th floor. Fire escape goes all the way to the roof, with reachable access to the kitchen window! It's turn-of-the-previous-century construction, with solid brick walls and recent sound-proofing throughout from the post-fire renovation a few decades ago. The brick exterior is the kind that inspires certain sorts of people to say "I could climb that!" The difference is, I can and do climb it often and with ease. All the way to my apartment window. Especially on evenings like tonight, when the overcast sky and rain help me avoid being spotted. I climb most of the way next to the fire escape, in case I need a quick reality-check for a random observer. Which is also why I use the fire escape regularly, so people see me there as a routine thing. As my flip-flops dangle from my belt carabiner, I quickly ascend up the wall. My 'claws' – for lack of a better term – combined with new talents like the creepy climbing-up-sheer-surfaces thing, make it practically effortless even on wet brick in the rain. Sometimes I forget what it was to be a human.

***

There were subtle changes at first, which were easily brushed aside due to the obvious changes in my life. I hadn't seen a reason to worry about a few bad dreams here and there. And with my food changes like all those damned vegetables, is wasn't really surprising that I started to really crave meat? I gave up a little sanity through all of that, and I used to blame those changes in my life for taking a toll on my disposition, not what I now know it had been. Do you know the saying

"Hindsight is 20/20?" Bingo. I had easily dismissed the moments of paranoia or short-fuse reactions, until one crazy thought got through and became "plausible" to me. Then another "plausible" scenario had wormed into my head. Soon I had trouble sleeping, but it wasn't my fault! The water in the neighborhood, the air quality, the security at the grocery store – all valid concerns, right? Not just for me, but what about my family? Wait, what about them? Were they to blame? The neighbors?! I became concerned for my wife. No, I actually became paranoid *about* my wife. Was she poisoning me? What about the kids?!

I had been in and out with doctors and specialists back then, I'd improved with dramatic physical success! I had lost thirty pounds overall, I had started sleeping more soundly...well, albeit for only a few hours instead of several. Didn't that mean that my suspicions had merit, though, if I was healthy? In retrospect I knew, I KNEW, that something else was wrong. But through my pride I easily denied the truth in favor of something easier for my ego to accept: It couldn't be me. It had to be 'them.' Or *her*. The first time my heart stopped beating, I was so afraid and full of rage I nearly tore myself apart along with the house. Luckily no one was home at the time. At least, until I realized I shouldn't still be ransacking the house after my heart had stopped. No matter what though, during the rampage, I had been sure something would have to be done to protect us from her. That was the day, after thankfully coming to my senses again, I realized I had to leave them. It was the best, most tragic, introspective, torturous decision I've ever made. After that, it's hard to feel guilty about much of anything.

***

Something that has helped me keep my sanity over the last couple years, and to make me feel more human still, is to sleep. Before all this happened, I loved to sleep. I used to practically hibernate nightly. I still love the idea of sleeping, it's just a lot lot lot harder now. I'm a different animal now. My perception abilities are so out of whack, that I battle with sleep nearly every night. From what I've gathered through research, as 'undead' (it's not MY choice of label!) I shouldn't need to sleep. And I probably don't need to, except that one of the ways I've maintained my 'humanity' is to have habits which keep me grounded like the rest of the species. The Human species. My former species. So I try, and pretty much fail, to sleep nightly. I do occasionally sleep, but it's for very short intervals. I don't often feel tired, either, which doesn't help. Sometimes I just case the apartment, catering to the paranoia. I had hoped that someday an intruder via the fire escape would be the perfect opportunity to feed my craving and see if I'm truly cursed. But the paranoia won't let me actually leave the place unsecured. I placed bars on the windows and main door so they can't be opened easily nor quietly. I put in security doors for the two bedrooms, with reinforced frames, amongst other crazy mods to the place. Of course, I set those doors to keep intruders stuck *in* the room, since I 'sleep' in the living room. On a mattress, on the floor... behind the futon. Which I plated with eighth-inch steel plate, ballistic gel padding, and slip-covers made from ballistic nylon fabric. Hey, it helps me sleep at night. It weighs a ton, but for me it's like moving a light chair. I just hope it doesn't fall through the floor someday. Of course, I also ran the same steel plate, with just the ballistic nylon wrap, behind the wainscoting I put around the room and on the back of the main door. I then added the same plate steel to a tall double-sided bookshelf-hutch thing I assembled (from Ikea no less!) which blocks direct line of sight or fire from the main door to most of the living room and kitchen. I could go on, but I think the message is clear – I don't really sleep, I'm paranoid, I have a background in construction and fabrication, and I like to work with my hands. If I were smarter I think I'd be Frankenstein or some other mad scientist. Maybe my next name will be Frank.

***

Like any other eating night, I settled into my routine of dinner, calves-brains casserole with a side of random raw meat, in front of the TV. Every few days I need to eat something it used to be, but time's been getting longer in-between. I eventually shut everything down and secured the apartment per my routine. As I set out my bag and wiped down the door handles, I was listening to Miss Thompson (up and over two apartments) and her boyfriend-of-the-week work out 'mutual frustrations' while April (apartment below me) snored softly on the couch with the TV still on. Energy pig. Devon's twins were out of bed and conspiring on their bedroom floor above my spare bedroom. I could hear him typing away at the keyboard in his office, down the hall. These were all the kinds of people that made tempting targets for a predator like me. They were overworked, weak, tired, distracted, annoying at times, and didn't really have many visitors. Of course, I also knew that they weren't the right targets for me. Well, April was right for me, probably both as a meal and as a lover. She was young, attractive, nerdy way beyond my understanding, played video games, rarely dressed up, and she ate takeout frequently. I may be a monster but I'm still a man, and I've been 'dead' from my family a long time. It's nice to think about human needs sometimes.

Technically, I'm still human. With only a few contentious points, that is. First, my heart doesn't beat implying death, but "death" is consistently defined as a 'permanent end of all life functions in an organism,' roughly paraphrased, which would indicate I am not "dead." It's always been a cyclical argument that helps put me to sleep sometimes.

***

I awake abruptly to a startled silence. I have earplugs in, serenity sounds playing from the mantle stereo, and an empty room. *Now what?* I smell something, though, a vanilla odor leeching into the room from the door. I scan but find nothing as I pull my earplugs. Immediately I hear a cacophony of clanking plastic on metal with undertones of slowly creaking boots, like the floorboards of an old boardwalk under foot. They're creaking on the floor, though, in the hallway right outside my door. It was muffled by a static noise, but not well enough as I focus on the sounds. There are four people in the hall, huddled not five feet from my door. I stifle a curse as the radios in the hall and outside my kitchen window (on the fire escape!) spout in unison orders being barked from the third person outside the door. The radio voice cuts a deep wound into my mind as they begin...

148

"No thermal signs from the apartment, sir. Recon confirms subject has not left, so we presume camouflaged from thermal. HQ presumes dangerous – but **capture** protocols are ordered. Bag and tag for analysis and let's go home people. I want to know what we've got before disposal."

Damn, not again. How did they find me? If it's them... I hear the heavy steel tube picked up from the floor as the hallway men crowd outside the door ready to charge in.

"Deet and Frost." the man continues to give orders on the move, "You're with me in through the apartment door. Al, sit on that fire escape in case he rabbits to you. Carla, if he gets past Al and to the roof, take him down. Volts preferably, I don't need a mess like last time! He should be out by now. On my mark..." I quickly shove the custom earplugs back in!

"Copy that, Jim" came the replies from the four other mechanical voices over some sort of muffled speaker. I could smell the tension and hear the build-up as activity tensed in the hallway and on the fire escape. "Mark!"

I raced toward the kitchen to grab my 'go bag' – a collection of all my identifiable gear, documents, and research data which was the one thing I could never just leave here. To many it would have seemed a tremendously heavy military duffel which was full of useless junk to most. To me, it held what was, what is, and what would be my life after this.

Admittedly, I'm an action buff like many guys, and I always find that people in the movies screw up worst by never having a plan, even when they know they should. I don't do "let's run upstairs and hide in the one-exit bathroom cowering in the tub" kind of scenario. I, have some very basic steps which we're about to literally run through!

I faintly hear the startled expressions as everyone outside the main door, planning on the door giving out easily, cram themselves into a door which is hardly bent now. *This isn't my first dance like this, morons!* So, here we go: Rule one, figure out *what* is here and *where* they are, specifically. I say what instead of 'who' because 'who' comes later when we have time to actually ponder those thoughts.

Rule two is pretty simple: Get the bag with your 'life' in it. Rule three is a little vague, but it's pick the best of the planned escape routes. Rule four is to execute rule three without hesitation. I do my best internal Yoda, "*Do, or do not. There is no try!*" I head toward the kitchen, where I've decided that the east kitchen window – away from the fire escape - is the best escape option. Of course, it's not an easy window to get through. The guy on the fire escape and his backup means the east side is covered. There are two to four about to burst in the main door on the west side of the apartment, which leaves south and east escapes. The bedrooms on the north side may already be compromised, which leaves the option to rabbit toward the balcony on the east side. It's the logical choice, so I clearly can't choose that path in front of me. "*Truly I have a dizzying intellect!*" I throw the duffel strap over my head and shoulder, grab the ends of the heavy bag, then launch it through the window a split-second in front of me then twist myself around as we crash through the shattering glass and drop slightly, grabbing onto the ledge and wall. I had the ledge but end up sliding down a little bit. The sounds of my claws in the brick, the rain of glass dancing along the building as it falls, and the distant cursing of snipers covering the balcony are painfully washed away as I hear the door, frame and all, explode in a thunderous impact right into the steel-lined hutch. I almost didn't hear the armed team storm into the living room as I scurried across and upward along the wall toward the corner and the roof.

Rule five is critical for anyone running away from just about anything, especially people with guns. *Zig Zag! Never escape in straight lines unless you can outrun them and anything they can shoot at you.* I start zigzagging as I shimmy toward the south side of the building, where the fire escape guys are still expecting me to head toward the roof. I can already hear Al swearing from around the corner, a story or two below now, as chunks of the wall start popping away in a dusty mix of glass and liquid and needles with cute little feathers falling away. *Are tranquilizers really like that? I thought that was just in the movies? Huh.* I can hear the two snipers over the balcony colorfully giving away my trajectory towards the roof over the radio. *Thanks guys! Hmmm. I wonder what Commander Jim meant by "should be out by now?"*

I slip around the corner of the building along the wall spotting the sniper on the roof across the street on the other side of the opposing building, where his vantage gave him a view of both the south and west sides of the building. *Glad I didn't go that way!* He turns toward me, luckily an awkward angle, positioning something that looks very intimidating as I launch myself toward the fire escape, smashing into it with a thud and a jerk as the duffel hammers across my knees and stops its acceleration at the fire escape. "Ow!" *that actually hurt!* Al, still a little below me, keeps his calm and checks if he has a shot, but then starts up the metal stairs after me. I move upward quickly, causing him to hasten his ascent, preternaturally dodging the noisy bullets which punch loud and odorous craters into the wall around me along with my duffel! Nothing more disturbing than bullet holes through my clothes and probably my notes, dammit!

Rule six now – if you're keeping track. *Don't do what you're expected to do.* They knew I would want to get to the roof – it's a plethora of options for cover, escape, shadowing, blocking sight-lines, and even the roof access door could get me back into the building if I wanted to do something truly insane! But that's why rule six is here. I leap up the side of the fire escape toward the roof again, letting Al close the distance while making his buddy miss as I contort to avoid more of the bullets. *How many do they have, I wonder?* Then I drop downward in a slide down the fire escape support bars, allowing the weight of my bag to drag me down in a 'controlled fall' of sorts. I fall right past Al, bless his heart.

"Sorry Al. Tell Jim I'll let him know when I can reschedule our coffee date!" I slide right out of any good angles for the sniper or Al;

and then actually fall right off the ten foot high section that was the bottom of the fire escape when the ladder isn't deployed. Right onto the pavement, on top of the duffel bag which had been dangling behind my knees. But I rebound spectacularly, slipping in the water with my bare feet, then half slide half propel myself right into the wall. "Dammit Al!" I yell upward as I hear the footsteps thundering down after me.

Al finished his tirade of colorful expletives and started reporting into his radio as I bolt across the street, through the alley toward Jackson street. I hang a left, sprinting now, taking me south southeast away from the apartment. Three blocks down the deserted street, I cross to my right heading through the dark and empty parking lot. Two more blocks west under the overpass. I cross south and travel another block, then scale the wall of a small mid-block brick building. I slink into the in-progress renovation area above Dave's Pawn Shop.

I force some nails back through the plywood boards after entering through the empty window frame. Then I fix the plastic sheeting, hoping it will help insulate and keep this area warmer. Then I get familiar with the layout of the place, before settling down and listening. There's no one in this or any of the nearby buildings, which confirms privacy I had hoped for. I had observed the area, but never come in here, specifically for Rule number seven: *Always have at least one escape destination that is quick, simple, not too far, and is completely separate from any trace back to your compromised identity.* You don't want to have any history with the destination, just in case the normally-inept authorities actually bothered to observe you before they tipped their hand. *They won't find me here! And they won't even try for at least a day or two!* First, they'll scour the airport, bus stations, train stations...etc, for any signs of me running. If they decide I haven't gotten away, they might start a search for me, but unlikely. *If they do, then I'll actually get out of town!*

Rule eight is the toughest: *Survival first, get questions answered later. Preferably from another State.* I'm already wondering, though! Who were they? How they found me? What did I screw up? *More importantly: Why weren't they more surprised or scared of a guy who jumps out windows and climbs across walls?* Al didn't seem surprised, which probably means that Deet, Frost, Carla, and Commander Jim probably knew about me already. I wasn't ready the last time someone came after me, and barely escaped. Hence the rules. But this time, I was listening! And one word stuck out from Al's radio report as I had run across the street: "Ghoul." It was clear. Now *that* makes me reevaluate Rule eight.

I'm suddenly very tired with a bitter, pasty taste on my tongue. I can feel myself becoming angry, losing control, but not enough to fall apart yet. *How odd,* I thought as I put in my earplugs, *that I'm actually tired or fatigued. Sleep, huh.* I pulled out the little pillow and the aptly-named 'mummy bag' to rest in. I don't seem to generate much of my own body heat any longer, which is why I can't live in the far North in the winters, so amongst the rather mundane items I carry is a large quantity heating elements like the ones people use to warm their hands or bums while hunting? Critical items in my case. If I have to sleep out in the cold, without these, I risk being so lethargic that someone could probably haul me off before I even noticed. *I'm so tired, now!* I set my bed in the darkest corner of the room, not worried about the sun with all the windows boarded up, then lean back with my mini-pen and note-pad to jot down my thoughts on the evening. Earplugs go in. Nose-plugs are a necessity around here, so those go in. I begin jotting down notes. Now I can start to figure things out. *Why am I so tired? I didn't find any darts in me? Did I inhale some fumes from one that popped in front of me? Was that static noise at the apartment some sort of pumped-in gas?* I write every thought and detail. They're necessary for my research. Maybe some day I'll be able to rejoin society? *I think my next ID will be "Bruce Banner." Wow, I'm not usually this tired...*

***

Five days ago, after waking up in the third-floor space above Dave's Pawn Shop, I decided to disregard rule eight, then nine by extension: *Get out of town and make it far away.* This wasn't the first time I had been under siege, but they hadn't been quite so close last time! These guys were at my home, knew me or of me, and had been prepared. That means they were either expecting someone else, maybe not some*thing* else, or they generally engage 'supernaturals' like me. *It was time,* I had told myself, *to find out who they were, what they were about, and how I fit into their agenda.* Oh, I could run again, but I decided to make a stand. If they knew about me, maybe they knew more about my condition? I'm a predator, after all, so maybe it's time I started acting like a ghoul and learn how to hunt? It was time to hunt the hunters. I came here to figure myself out and take the next step in my journey. I came here to kill a human, then satisfy my hunger. Maybe these hunters are what I need to really take that next step? I'm a freakin GHOUL! It was time to start acting like it.

It hadn't taken long to figure out who they were, over the last few days. My apartment was crawling with forensic analysts from the Sheriff's office and Feds too. There were about a hundred people with nothing better to do lounging about in a crowd watching the cops work. I had lingered around the street beneath my apartment building, watching, avoiding any of my neighbors as they came or went. For the most part I just watched as Fed nerds meticulously cataloged and picked up glass shards and debris, while talking about trying DNA matching to some serial killer wanted for murders most recently from Ohio. I had never been to Ohio! Or had I? But then I had heard him: *Commander Jim.* He had walked right out the front double-doors where I could, with difficulty, listen in on one side of his phone conversation. I'm not Superman, so I had to work really really hard to focus my attention on the one conversation, standing in a crowd of gawkers, but it had gone roughly like this...

"...definitely a Ghoul or a Vampire, McSween. Probably a ghoul, seemed like a newb. Feeding himself raw meat we found in the fridge. No blood-lust nor bodies found. Neighbors liked the guy and say he's been here four months and works during the day in construction somewhere around here. And no ego."

"Ego?" I presume came from the phone.

"Yes sir," he said, "usually the Vamps come at us until they're hurt *then* they try to run. This one grabbed a bag, jumped out a window, and then ran wee wee wee all the way home."

The phone blurted out more but I couldn't make it out. *Vampires? W.T.F? Seriously?*

"Understood sir. Janey believes that this might be the same thing our team was chasing in Albuquerque earlier this year. We never got this close, but the patterns seem similar. If we are tracking a Vamp, he must be really different or making little friends to distract us when we get close. In either case, this doesn't feel like the guy from Ohio. I think" More from the other end, then "No sir, I haven't dismissed anything. It could be that it's a coincidence that we stumble on two Supers in the same area. Isn't the first time. Might be one is using the other as a smokescreen, too. Either way sir, we'll bag him if he sticks around or if he tries to get out of town. Surveillance is already combing satellite imagery and setting up around town here to see what we can find."

He looked tense as the phone rambled on for a bit. I noticed because he was scanning the crowd now, and I'd had to divert my stare before he noticed me focused on him. I tried to be discreet about checking around me for agents pouring into the crowd. I didn't see any. *Phew!* I turned back toward him as he was setting his gaze on me, but luckily a young woman sidled up to his side drawing his attention momentarily. I don't know if I hid my fear and surprise well, but he paused for the slightest of moments at me and then continued his visual scanning of the crowd.

"Janey's here right now, sir. I'll send you what we get asap. If we're going to keep the locals in the dark, then I should go. They're getting pretty restless around here and I'm standing in a crowd of the eggheads collecting evidence. Tell Maria she owes me a batch of cookies whenever I get back."

He hung up the phone, sighed rather forcefully, then turned to the young redhead at his side. He seemed to tower over her with his tall, thin build, but was only marginally taller and very unimposing. Roughly six-two versus her five-eight, I'd estimate. He had the look of a determined man who preferred his books to people, and even more-so when it came time to actually talk to the opposite sex. He was already visibly flustered, at least to me, just standing there next to her. He was tired, unshaven, and looked as if he'd been eating fast food far longer than his body's acceptable threshold. He wasn't a slob, he just looked like a weathered man, around my age but with a lot more wear and tear than I've had. His voice was even a little hoarse, adding to his aura of beaten-down man. *But I know looks are often deceiving!*

"Looks like he was planning to stay, Janey" he said awkwardly but quickly found his rhythm, "we found the obvious stuff, but he had a crate full of surveillance equipment in the bedroom with a receipt from over a month ago! Never set it up. Talked with his neighbors, working not too far away? Doesn't seem like our guy. I can't believe it's this disciplined and was prepared! This guy had a grab-bag ready. Tell me what I'm missing? What links them, Janey?"

Her voice was playful, like a smarmy teacher who snickered as she told you the lessons for the day, enjoying that you were too busy watching her than listening to what she said. "Definitely not the guy from Ohio, boss." She nudged into him playfully, adjusting her glasses innocently, "I'm thinking Ghoul for sure, who likes Abba and the Beatles at the same time. Probably a Taurus! Our guy from Ohio is obviously a Gemini."

"Janey," he said as he pinched between his eyes and pulled his head back, "McSween is all up my butt on this presumed Vamp from Ohio. If this isn't him, can you just get me the facts and let me go get some shut-eye before I have a fatal accident while cleaning my gun?"

"Sorry sir, but you know how boring these guys are. I may be a mega-nerd, but I actually like things other than comic books and Sci-fi conventions! Anyway, footprints don't match. M.O isn't consistent with the last time we got close. Al said he sounded like a

Midwesterner, not like a southerner, and *this* guy was scared enough to put in his defenses and then still run! Maybe we discovered a new species? We could call it a ghoul-nerd!" He just stared at her pleadingly. "Okay, If Ohio was in there when we hit it like we did, with the defenses in that apartment, he would have torn us up real bad. Oh, and this guy has that bed behind the futon, which was armored by the way! I don't think he wants to give up being human. How tragic! I think he's trying to stay a man - not become the thing we all expect, considering all the patterns I see here. Maybe it's just me, but you might actually be able to talk to this guy this time, learn something, before you decide to just put a few rounds between his eyes." She looked at him like an adorable puppy dog, but got silence and an empty stare in return. "Go get your nap, boss. We've got this. We'll call if we need you or find out anything worth mentioning. You're only a half-mile away." She was young except for her eyes, deeper and older than the rest of her shell gave away. She was attractive with fair, freckled skin, and had the sexy 'lab coat with the glasses and hair-pulled-back' thing going on. I thought about that classic male fantasy scene where she takes off the glasses, slowly shakes down her hair as she lets it out of its restraint, then opens her lab coat to expose her perfect body wrapped in lingerie just for me. And then I eat her delicious brain.

Unfortunately, that's how my fantasies end these days.

I never went back to my apartment building. I'd spent days tracking and assimilating knowledge of this band of assailants. I got pictures from a super-zoom-something-or-other camera from the pawn shop. I could recognize their faces, their scents, and even their voices now. They were easy to track and observe, arrogant in their autonomy it seemed. *Except for her!* I could have followed Janey around for the next year I think, but I decided I was already creeping myself out with the super-stalker thing! Interestingly, they were staying at four different hotels surrounding the area in what probably amounted to some sort of quick-response net or grid for spotting me or this other fellow from Ohio. They had set up some kind of sensors in the last day, which brought me nervously to the conclusion that I needed to speak with Jim now, if I was going to do it, before we have more evening escapades if they're able to track me somehow. *Besides, I can leave the evening escapades for Frost and the guy hiding out in his hotel room. I don't see how he could be ready at a moment's notice with all their tiring activity.* If I corner and speak to Jim quickly, in a random setting without incident, maybe I can reason with him. Maybe they'll let me go or ask for my help? Or at least I may find out more of what he knows about my condition. Maybe he'll just kill me on the spot? "Maybe" just isn't cutting it anymore. I need answers.

***

I had followed Jim this morning to a new boutique coffee shop between his hotel and Al's dive of a motel. I should see him still in line but he's nowhere to be found. I step out of line to scan the seating area off to the right of the line, and step right in front of a rapidly moving carry-tray of 4 coffee beverages which serves as an impact zone between me and the woman who was chasing it toward the door. So much for those great spidey-senses! One of the cups opens up on impact, spilling onto the front of my dress shirt and splatters down my jeans onto my shoes. The other cups crash to the floor as the red-head bounces off me and lurches backward to the floor, landing harshly right on her rear.

"Oh my, are you okay miss?" I ask as she *Janey!* looks up at me with a disheveled look from behind her crooked glasses. *Still wearing that lab coat, I see!*

"Oh no. Oh God, I'm so sorry sir. It's all over your shirt! Are, are... are you okay? I'm such a klutz!" I stand there dumbfounded at this serendipitous encounter. "I don't seem to have any on me, but you... Oh I hope you're not mad. I swear it was an accident..."

I extend a hand out to her and romantically say "Up?" *Idiot!*

She looks up at me, as my brain screams *"RUN!"* from behind the curtain, and smiles the most melting yet nervous smile. Then she took my hand.

I tried not to shiver as the sensation of her touch actually sent chills, or the equivalent for a ghoul, down my spine. I feel like a nervous teen suddenly as my creep-o-meter red-lines internally as I'm just staring at her. "I'm so sorry miss. I stepped right out in front of you. Are you okay? Let me buy you replacement coffees, it's the least I can do?! How thoughtless of me!" I help her up then start gathering up the shattered beverages on the floor as she stands over me, hopefully not noticing how often I have to check out her legs atop her leather boots. Luckily two of the beverages actually survived the drop!

"Only if you let me buy you one for running into you" she blurts out with a half-giggle at the end.

"Of course" I reply, as I stand up and lock eyes with her for that existential moment which seems to never end. "Always say yes when a lovely woman offers to buy you a drink, I say!" *What the hell was that?! Smooth-o-meter just dropped below zero.* I can't get a sense of her as all I can smell is coffee from my shirt compounded by all the sounds in here causing interference in my head.

Thankfully, before I say anything else so debonaire, a young employee whisks around from the back with a mop and bucket, telling us "We can replace the dropped beverages, no cost, miss! We're very sorry for the inconvenience, sir, as well. We have a restroom toward the back if you'd like to clean up." He mops up the spills in no time and puts one of those little yellow triangle signs over each of the wet spots. "We'd be happy to get you a complimentary beverage of your choice, as well, sir." He starts back toward the counter, "Oh, what were the other two beverages, miss?"

She continues to keep her eyes connected to mine this whole time, and responds "Double-Cacao with Cinnamon Caffe's, I think. Well, um, that's what they all were. So it's easy to remember."

She's smiling again and looks away, a slight flush in her cheeks. "I'll take one of those too!" I'm probably still staring at her. "Looks like you won't have to buy me one after all! Sounds like the day is starting off well, sort of." I decide to bite the bullet. "Would you like to stay for a bit, with me? I could grab some bagels or something? I'd love to have a conversation with you."

"Oh, I'd love to!" She bites her lower lip and frowns. "Except that I have another date. I mean, I have four coffees." I smile what I think is a charming smile of acceptance. "No!" She goes on."What I mean is, I don't have another date. I have to be somewhere. Not like I wouldn't stay. It's not like I have to 'wash my hair' or something. What I mean is! Ugh." She takes a slow, deep breath. "I have a meeting and I have to deliver the coffees, that's why I can't stay. But I want to! Phew that was hard. Rain check?"

"I think I get it. It's fine. I probably should go wash my clothes anyway."

She looks like she's suddenly about to cry! "I said I was sorry" she says sheepishly.

"Oh! I didn't mean it that way. I just..." *What was I thinking? Jerk!*

"Ha! Got ya!" She smiles at me, with a prodding finger. "I'm serious about the rain check." She grabs a drink handle-wrap-thingy and writes down a number. She hands it to me as the young employee returns and hands us our beverages. "Call me! I'm Janey, by the way. Well, Jane but everyone calls me Janey. Long story. I'll tell you when we meet for coffee, if you want to know."

Crap! What name am I supposed to give her?! "How thoughtless of me" I stall "my name is Matt. It's a pleasure to make your acquaintance. I will definitely call you!"

She stalls long enough to search me for insincerity, but seems satisfied and rushes out the door with her coffees again. I head for the restroom to rinse out my shirt. Dried coffee in a blue button-down probably won't come out well. Luckily I don't sweat any longer! *New*

My Life In Drool

Rule: Never visit the places you know are frequented by the enemy. Probably shouldn't make dates with them either.

***

The coffee shop is even louder and more erratic as I walk out from the restroom. I take one last quick sweep, wondering if Commander Jim was aware of a tail and used the door into the mall area. I guess it's just as well; I never would have kept up with him in the the mall or along the riverside boardwalk. "No thanks, maybe next time!" I mutter quietly, as I put my sunglasses on and spin toward the door.

"It's too bad, I think she really likes you. And probably a good thing she didn't know who you were, otherwise this would have been messy, Ghoul." And there he was, Commander Jim had been standing just inside the entrance right behind me, now only three feet from me, smiling a toothy and devious smile. I imagine similar to what Red Riding Hood saw when the Wolf spoke to her. "You should know I tag all my agents and often listen in when I think they're with a suspicious individual - especially when I know we're being tailed. I'm just disappointed that you were this easy to grab." I can smell the fury and see the agitation in his movements. Not to mention his temperature is spiked. He's agitated and over the edge I think.

"Jim! Look, I think we should talk. I'm not who you're looking for. I've never even been to Ohio..." I try to smile and reason with him, even as I start to feel myself losing control, inexplicably reacting to his emotional state. Whatever passes for Ghoul adrenaline starts firing all my muscles and I fight hard to keep from twitching myself. "Janey got the right impression of me!"

"Oh, I know *she* thinks you're someone I should talk to. Problem is, *I* know exactly how dangerous and deceptive you things are. You want to talk, okay? You come with me now, quietly, and I'll be sure to visit you in your holding cell for all the conversation you want." His eyes narrowed even further, accentuating his menacing look. "Otherwise, things get messy. I've had plenty of time, during your little exchange,

161

to get my teams in place. Running won't do anything for you." He moves his hand toward where a gun would be...

"Jim! Let's sit and have a coffee. Here, take mine!" I shuffle pass the hot beverage to him, making him reflexively block or catch. By the time he gets his hands clear I'm halfway toward the exit to the rest of the building and the mall area. I can hear his issuing of orders, presumably into a radio, so I'm sure they know where I'm going. Hopefully, he was bluffing about having his teams in place. *Definitely time for rule ten about staying away from enemy hangouts.*

As I bound down the mall office hallway from the coffee shop, I don't see agents nor anyone blocking the hallway. Obviously, he must have been bluffing if he didn't have even this door blocked! I roll through the doors into the mall area and reel as the noise level from the empty hallway into the mall area explodes in my head. I bounce off a jewelry booth in the middle of the walkway, distracted by the cacophony of sensory input, before I can even open my eyes. I rip off one of the wooden rods holding up its makeshift roof and jam it into the door handles to delay Commander Jim's pursuit. I have the distinct feeling that I should avoid any direct action with him, at least for now.

Problem number one with the decision to run this way: while I know *about* this mall, I've never actually been *to* this mall. I can see that I'm actually on the second floor, while the coffee shop was on the first floor outside. *Great!* I take off to my right, moving just a little faster than the crowds, trying to make it a little harder to spot me. I'm near the end of the hall when I spot two groups of SWAT-looking individuals rounding both corners ahead of me, sweeping both walkways back toward me, causing people to crowd in the few channels that cross between the openings to the lower floor. A few of them hold up photos against people as they clear the way. *Time to improvise!* I jump over the railing, which keeps people from falling through the opening while looking down upon the lower level, and dig my claws into the walls as my flip-flops drop to the crowd below. I then scurry along the inside wall, hopefully out of view of the teams moving this way above me. I head back in the direction I came from, jump back up onto the second floor only long enough to pass the broken jewelry booth and jump down into the next opening, crawling along the inner wall and then slipping down to crawl upside-down along the ceiling above first floor. *I never had the nerve to even try this! I'm freakin' Spider Man! Probably would be cooler if I didn't leave claw tracks in my wake.* Unfortunately, the teams on first floor spot my ceiling-crawling but are hindered by the crowd which is thicker and less budging than second floor. And it seems like they haven't been given permission to open fire. *Yet, that is.*

Someday I'll learn to keep my thoughts to myself. "There he is!" bellows from below, causing people in the crowd to start screaming as the ceiling around me is popping with familiar glass needles and holes from far more damaging munitions. They're accompanied by the echoes of deafening explosions from the barrels of the guns almost disorienting me. I practically run on all fours, hanging upside down, along the ceiling back toward what I presume is the center of the mall. All the way I amazingly dodge bullets and needles from below, keeping ahead of the thundering heavy boots above me. The boots are mimicking the pounding in my head, which feels like an ape crashing again and again against its cage walls. The occasional barrel protruding over the edge, lets me know that it's not time to try going back up top. *Well, at least I'm keeping focus, though.*

As I scurry into the center area, I slide up to the second floor at the far side, and look for something to the upper levels I see in this section. The glass-encased elevator is right next to me, with the escalators back across the center where a collection of armed personnel is massing as the hallways converge together. The crowd here has started to gather over there, to see what the commotion is, further inhibiting them. I burst up the glass wall outside the elevator tube. *Probably not the smartest idea, braniac!* Shots from across the way begin punching holes in the rapidly fracturing glass, and the glass above and around me shatters, dropping me few feet until I grab the metal frame that rims glass. Fresh pieces of glass dig deep into my forearms and hands, sending more ghoul-adrenaline which excites my system even further. I feel something happening to my body, physically, but I can't worry about that right now! I jump across, inside the tube, and scurry up the far side to where the shaft ends above. I shatter the glass next to this level and jump out, swinging around the wall and onto the fourth floor, heading toward the dutifully well-marked Exit sign.

As I burst into the stairs, I see a helicopter, descending along the outside of the mall area windows, leaving the exact area I'm hoping to get to! Hopefully, I'll make the roof before they figure out where I'm going. I saw no spotters on the sides of the Huey, so hopefully they didn't see me entering the stairwell! Something makes me hesitate, and I stop mid-step as I'm bounding toward the roof. A lurch of nausea doubles me over, as my system reminds me just how hungry I am for some adequate sustenance. Luckily, I breathe and focus it away quickly, my mind winning over my stomach this time. I start ascending again, but now I'm crushing the stair-rail every time my hand grabs it on the way up. There is a little bit of joy in the back of my mind with that, but again, I'll have to worry about that later.

I've mentioned that I run fast. I make it up the six flights of stairs to the roof door faster than an Olympian runs the 220m. I, however, don't get winded nor have a heartbeat to be pounding in my chest like I would have years ago. Of course, I don't really seem to need to breathe, so maybe it's not a fair comparison.

Reaching the top landing, I hit the solid roof door hard, only to realize the laws of physics still don't quite bend just for me. The door bends outward but doesn't open, and I nearly spill back over the rail down the center of the stairs as it rejects me with an equal but opposite amount of energy. I'm sure that hurt, but I'm pretty frantic myself now, feeling like cornered prey. I stop to listen and hear the tell-tale signs of armed personnel jostling and hustling up the stairs. I take a risky glance over the edge as I massage my shoulder and see the occasional barrel, with cliché flashlights on in here, four-plus flights below. *Time to get the hell out of here, NOW!* I back up to the top of the stair landing and launch myself at the door once again, crushing the door outward this time, along with probably my shoulder and clavicle too.

My Life In Drool

The door and I tumble out onto the roof in explosive chaos. It's premature, but I smile as I 'taste the free air.'

***

I feel the sun burning into my slightly-balding head as I spot my cap ten feet away. I shakily get up from the crushed rooftop door, making sure I've got all my limbs intact. The buildings roof engines are running while birds are all flapping haphazardly away from my entrance. I head toward my cap and feel a sting in my back mid-section as a reddish vapor dissipates in front of me which barely misses spattering my cap. The noise is deafening even as a new, second splatter does hit the hat. I turn, just short of the cap, toward the source of deafening noise behind me. Standing next to the wall beside the shattered doorway, next to the resting tranquilizer rifle which I recognize from her hotel room, is Carla. She's holding a menacingly large pistol at me as a small metal object tings on the ground next to a similar one at her feet.

Oh God, she just shot me. Twice. I put my hands up in front of me, palms toward her as my legs buckle, dropping me to my knees. There's a strange and exhilarating pounding in my chest, like a death knell pounding harder and faster and harder and faster. I feel the overwhelming nausea of hunger again, accompanied by Vertigo as my brain cries out *"No! I'm not ready to die!"* internally. A feral presence creeps into my being, and I am actually welcoming to the release of control. *Why fight it?* I rationalize, *I don't really want to be present for my own death, anyway.*

She steps forward, the barrel ominously leveled at my head. I can feel my eyes start rolling back into my skull as I fight a losing battle over self-control. She stops just out of reach, raises both arms in a flippant gesture to match her smirk, and says "I'm sorry, but I just didn't remember to bring any tranq ammo this time." She gestures at the rifle. "Oops!" All I can think about is the hunger and the dark clouds swarm around the edges of my vision. I realize it's not vertigo as the clouds of darkness descend across my eyes. I feel at peace.

165

Catalino Tolejano, II

The darkness of death feels like a dream. I hear an explosion nearby, and can smell the mix of blood and gunpowder, but I'm all alone in the darkness. A surreal face flashes into view, like a flashlight being waved around randomly. Then the head stops in front of me, but it's not a head, it's a bowling ball with its holes with two on the top like eyes and the third where the nose would be. *Is death some sort of delirious shadow game? Maybe I'm just passed out and not dead yet?* From the dark void next to me, a swirling vortex of shadow coalesces into a monstrous humanoid form with an indistinguishable face. It grabs the throat I hadn't even seen below the bowling ball and tears it away from the weeble-wobble body which had been attached to the bowling ball. For an instant, I thought I heard the bowling ball cry out, but bowling balls don't talk! The bowling ball and body roll forward, yet the ball is still looking at me. I watch, stricken with fear at the rage and hatred emanating from the shadow monster next to me, as he brings a monstrous left arm down on the lilting form and grabs the top holes of the bowling ball. Then, bracing the lower hole with the right hand I hadn't even seen, it tears the bowling ball in half and rears its head back in a silent howl of triumph, as the weeble-wobble figure slumps to the darkness below us. Suddenly the shadow is looking down at me with its featureless face, upside down as I'm now the bowling ball, unable to move or react to the fear that overwhelms me. It leans down slowly, enjoying my terror, and forms a terrible maw of shadow fangs and gnashing teeth, drooling right into my eye as I lie helpless and unable to even blink. *Bowling balls don't have eyelids,* I tell myself. The sheer terror continues to overtake me as I feel its grip on my right shoulder, a clawed arm caressing along my form from my belly to my chin, and its excitement as the maw drops past my forehead just out of view. In the darkness I can tell it's crying blackened shadow tears. *Crocodiles shed tears while they eat their prey, don't they?* And then everything is bright and white, like the blinding sun on a clear day. I can smell the stink of humanity all around me and feel the shivering of my body, and I practically taste the fear from the darkness. *I'm not dead, yet?*

I'm sticky and soaked again. I open my eyes barely a sliver as the unforgiving sun reflects off the surfaces around me, blinding me like the light of my dream. I can feel wetness drying at my hands and mouth, and I smell the blood before I see it, splattered across my chest and arms all down my torso. I'm hunched over a pool of blood, which appears to be dripping out the corners of my mouth. *Oh no. I remember now, I'm shot. I'm dying on this damned roof! Carla killed me!* I reach up and feel a gouge in the side of my head, wiping away a black and bloody powder that stinks of sulfur. *Gunpowder? She shot me in the head! But I'm not dead. Okay, now what?* I bring a blood-soaked arm up to block the Sun's torturous glare and look for Carla, spinning on my heels as I stay in the catcher's stance. I zigzag my head awkwardly to avoid it being an easy target, again. I don't have to look far. She's face down, inches from where my heels were, the smoking gun at her side with a spent casing melting partly into her wrist, smoldering a little still. I can smell the blood, the burning flesh, the gunpowder, and her hair conditioner as I draw a long dark hair from my teeth. I'm suddenly elated to be alive but nauseated at the same time as I look down at the carnage before me. We're now on the opposite side of the door opening, hidden behind the access tower. *What the hell happened?* There's no pounding in my chest any longer, but it feels like high-voltage current is coursing through my whole body. *God I feel... alive!* I shiver as the near-orgasmic sensation erupts from my feet to my head, practically knocking me off my feet. Her skull is open and hollowed out on top, surrounded by a few large pieces of skull like the small fragments scattered about my hands and arms. The meat of her throat is missing, the source of most of the blood pool. Her head flashes the image of a torn bowling ball and I keel over forward in fear and self-loathing. My brain wants to vomit but my body denies giving up its prize. I look down to see a few pieces of brain matter underfoot and between my fingers. I instinctively lick the rest off my hands, discovering perhaps the greatest sensation I may have EVER felt or tasted. I stand and howl, head reared back, the scream of someone who just discovered true nirvana! I lean over the edge, peering down toward the boardwalk, and curse myself for denying myself all those delicious people. I scorn myself for not having the courage to do this sooner! *What am I doing?! I don't want to be the monster they think me to be.* I start to sob, dry tears being all that this crocodile can offer, as the guilt of taking her life sets in. Luckily, I don't have much time to think about it.

I hear the feds shouting to each other as they hit the top of the landing. I stand and clutch at the bullet holes of my shirt, wondering how badly I'm hurt, applying pressure like you see in all the movies. *How bad is it?* I find no wounds beneath the shirt. *It's a miracle! The brains are a freakin' miracle! I'm invincible! I could take on the world right now!* This feeling is magnificent, but I know it's time to go. *No wonder Jim thinks I'm so dangerous, I can see how people, Ghouls I mean, would become addicted to this. This must be like crack for serious users.* My instincts jump-start my brain again. *TIME TO GO!* I take two steps toward my hat from the rooftop corner, sweeping it and my sunglasses on as two men, machine guns nose-down, come around the corner. Apparently they were not expecting me to be there. They spot the dead woman on the ground and look up to see me moving toward them, probably all a-glow and wide-eyed in my excitement. They start firing in unison before they even get the barrels moving upward. My mind is like a fighter jet right now, streaking by as these snails slowly go about their day. I have time to notice their features, like their pale faces and dread expressions behind their goggles. They look like death has already come for them. I can smell and practically taste their fear, even with their weapons riddling the rooftop with bullets. I can tell so much about them that it frightens me, as well. *I didn't come here to be a monster. I came to find out what happens if I feed. To find out if I can be a man in control, not some sort of ravager of people. Do they deserve to die?* I step between the barrels, time moving in slow motion for me, right between them as their eyes widen even further in horror behind their goggles. I bring my clawed hands up to their eyes, and pat them on the cheeks simultaneously with a "Tsk! Tsk!" and a smile followed by a little scratch on their outer cheeks. I slide sideways between them, then turn and launch myself off the roof toward the river below, before they even begin to spin around toward me. Their eyes track me as bullets still fly out of the guns in a deafening cacophony of small explosions, working their way off the roof in the opposite direction. I hear myself chortling all the way down, too caught up in the experience to let the bullets whizzing by from below, wreck this experience! The murky water and swirls of colors within look inviting as I descend. Even as I extend into a feet-first dive, I feel no fear from the water below. The impact seems inconsequential as the water and the current sweep me in underwater loops, rapidly dragging me away from the mall area and away from them all. Away from her. I open my eyes to the murky darkness, black and quiet, and literally just roll with the current for a while. I can feel the cold of the water on my skin. As I roll, I wonder where I'll end up after this. I wonder if Ohio is nice this time of year? *I should really call Janey and tell her I can't meet her... Or maybe I should meet her now.* I smile as the current carries me through the darkness.

Catalino Tolejano, II

*Floundering in obscurity and the call of several comic-induced dreams of avarice, **Catalino Tolejano, II** lives in Southeastern Wisconsin along with his wife and son, deep behind enemy lines of great friends and phenomenal family. Held together by an eclectic plethora of entertainment ranging from his original Atari 2600 to Netflix and Blu-ray on the PS3, the Tolejano family manages to survive by foraging on organic foods and the frequent infusion of life-sustaining pizza, fast food, or take-out! Catalino frequently raids M&M stockpiles, comic/toy/gamer conventions, and the occasional triathlon event; further contaminating his mind with material for future stories.*

First Kill

Patrick A. Waldoch

First Kill

"You did pretty well today for your first practical shooting contest Mr. Garrett." I praise my young midshipman and acting quartermaster as we both start packing away our gear from the contest.

"Thanks Captain. I've been doing the drills and practicing on my off time at the armory until I swear my fingers bled. I was so nervous, I was sure I was going to forget something trying to keep track of so many different things, breathing properly, focusing on the front sight, finding the targets. I'm surprised my score wasn't at the very bottom."

This was Danny's first time shooting under pressure of a scenario, and not just at the armory's ballistics range. Even I'm surprised that he did so well too. About mid-pack in the scoring for a first-timer. Targets at a range are never the same as a practical shoot, but then again combat isn't the same as a practical shoot, but its closer than just a target range.

"Captain, I've got a question for you." he asks me with an almost schoolboy look to his face. Between his already boyish blonde curls and now his pie-eyed look on his face I'd swear he's a teenager.

"Shoot. No pun intended."

"Huh. Oh." He flustered a bit. "I was just wondering if I can look at your gun."

"Sure." I clear the magazine and cycle the slide to pop the round out of the chamber and hand it over to him.

I hear this is a pretty old gun and its been in your family for generations?"

"Yeah. It's been in the family since the 1960's or so."

"Wow! That's over two centuries!" Now he really looks like a teenager. All he needs are freckles. "Has it seen real combat? Like in battles and such? Uh I I mean, um, before you got it?" He starts to demure as he realizes he's thinking about the fact I executed my former 3rd officer not too long ago right here on this hanger deck in front of most of the crew for treason to the ship and her crew.

"Military issued Colt 1911A1 with extensive modifications since it waas made. It was issued to an ancestor of mine during the Vietnam War back on Earth in the pre-colonization days. I was told it saved the life of my ancestors as he used it in combat for the first time when his gunnery crew was about to get overrun by some North Vietnamese forces. It was the first time he had to kill anyone that part of the story I do remember. It's been used a few times since then." It's saved my hide more than once that's for sure.

"Can I try it Captain?" He's got that goo-goo eyes look again.

I sigh and break the bad news to him. "Another time. I need to get cleaned up and I believe you're on duty when the next watch starts, which is in five minutes."

"Oh crap!" as he realized the time. "Thanks Capt!" as he grabs his bag and runs off pell-mell down the corridors out of the hanger.

As I get my gear sorted and I'm finally headed out of the hanger, my first officer meets up with me in the hallway. "Captain, we're ready for the fold to the Farbrook colony as soon as we get back into the gravity well, which should be with in the hour. We said we'd be back around this time, so they should be expecting us but I had navigation try to plot us an emergence point somewhere at about the northern polar magnetic region to hide us just in case." Good thinking, knew I had a good first officer. "That's a good idea. This may be a neutral colony but with the way things have been escalating these last months, better to play it safe. In fact tell the helm to plan on a sweep

176

around the planet twice and have the MEGS station do a full sensor sweep to make sure no one else is around once we emerge. We should have enough reaction mass for the thrusters."

"Yes we're down to to 15% but that's more than enough to sweep the planet. Barely enough to make planet fall and blast out again should we have to abort though."

"Lets not have to abort then after making planet fall. Make sure that sweep is through. I'll be in my quarters. Take the conn and get us to the fade-out point and I'll be back before we make the fold. I need to clean up." I order him just as we reach my quarters.

* * *

"Emergence from fold-space is complete. Commencing planetary sweep." the nav-station crewman cries out.

"Ms. Yvette, contact the hanger deck to launch our comms-net satellites." A colony this size may only have a satellite or two for it's own communications between settlements and since the Bootlegger is too large for the main colonies' landing field with other ships there, l'll have her land near the town, unload the crew going on shore leave, and have Johnny take the ship out a few hundred klicks away to the ocean to suck down some needed water for the drive systems and stores.

"Getting a signal from the planet Captain. It coming from the capital city. They are requesting information as to who we are and our intentions." Pipes up Lisa at the comms station.

"Please reply with our standard greeting package and turn on our IFF transponder so they can read us. Also inform them that I personally will be making planet fall ahead of the Bootlegger to visit Governor Edgerton at the Farbrook government center to negotiate for some needed supplies."

"As ordered, Captain."

"All looks well in hand here to me. Mr. Samuels, you have the conn. Take care of my ship, if you please. Mrs. Yvette, please contact Misters Garrett and Green and tell them they are to meet me in the hanger deck. We'll be taking a shuttle down planet side to visit the Governor to negotiate some supplies while the Bootlegger continues her sweep."

***

With an uneventful planet-fall and docking, Chief Nate, Danny and I manage to get the local version of a taxi cab ground effect car to take us to meet with Governor Edgerton at the colony's government building at Settlement One without any major issues. With three settlements already you'd think they could come up with something better than 'Settlement One' as a name by now. We've been here a few times, and it's still called Settlement One.

As we walk inside the building looking for the Governor's office, Danny keeps fingering the butt of his pistol, same polymer thing he was shooting earlier today in the hanger, but I'm glad he's comfortable enough to carry it planet side. Nate, on the other hand, is a walking weapon and mini-armory. He's armed himself with two of his own pistols, a mil-spec rifle slung over his shoulder with extra magazines on his vest and belt, a few visibly large knives and God only knows whatever else secreted on his person, not to mention whatever he's got in the small knapsack he's carrying. Sensei has had a saying passed down to him from his martial arts teachers going back centuries which covers his philosophy: Karate is for when all the bullets have been shot, all the knives thrown, all the chairs are broken and all the ashtrays have been smashed. I've learned a lot from him but I kept it down to just two pistols on my gun-belt with some extra mags, and a single hidden knife in my boot. I may be paranoid but I'm not that paranoid.

The building is new since the last time we made a stop on

Farbrook so it took us some time, but we reached the Governor's secretary's desk after a small bit of wandering around like lost sheep. "Captain Marlene Pritchard of the Private Yacht Bootlegger, here to see Governor Kyle Edgerton the 3rd on personal business." I say to the man behind the desk.

"Ah yes, Captain Pritchard, Mr. Edgerton's been expecting you when he learned of your emergence from fold-space. Unfortunately he's still busy with government business and can't see you right now. He begs that you wait for him to finish and he'll meet you just as soon as he's able." The man gets up and starts directing us towards a waiting room nearby. "Please if you'll come this way I can offer you refreshments and a more comfortable place to wait for Mr. Edgerton."

He leads us to a nicely apportioned library with a warm and inviting feel to it with the hand crafted local woods and plenty of old fashioned books. Even in our modern day of electronics, simple bound and printed books still have a nostalgia and ambiance that just can't be replaced. And, it has plenty of comfortable sofas and chairs. Just the place for a nice short nap. I've been up too long already.

"If you need anything please just ring the comm pad on the wall or on the desk and I'll be right over." says our temporary host as he shuts the double doors behind him.

"Alright, where's the whiskey?" asks Nate as he starts searching the wet bar for something to drink.

"Whiskey?" Danny inquires as he makes his way over to the bar. "Isn't it a bit early in the day to start drinking?"

"It's nearly noontime by local reckoning, but its fifth watch already by ship's time and I've already stood three of them counting the tournament. Here it is. The good stuff."

"How do you know its the good stuff?"

"Because it was hidden in back of the lower cabinet away from the other bottles, that's why." He begins to pour out three drinks. "Here you go kid, drink up. It will put some hair on your chest. Here you go Marlene, hopefully it won't put hair on yours."

"Thanks." I reply dryly to him. "I hate to have to shave my breasts using your razor."

We all settle back and just relax and enjoy the comfort. Danny turns on the display unit and gets just one vid channel. We're in the outback of the known galaxy. While we can move between whole star systems with a really good telescope, navigation computer and a fold drive, faster than light communications only happens by courier ships, so the only broadcast is the local planetary station. Nate tosses back his drink and immediately kicks back for a nap. The vid is going on about some ruckus at newest colony established on the planet just a year ago and some disputed land rights issues that's gotten out of hand. I'm guessing that's the fire Kyle's still trying to put out. I decide it's time for my nap as well.

"Captain, can I ask you a personal question?" So much for the nap. Kid's got that look again.

"Depends Danny, what's the question? "

"You've got the various shooting competitions going on-board and all that for us to practice our combat skills and stuff but what about when the real thing happens?"

"That's when your training takes over. We practice because most of the time people don't rise to the occasion but fall back onto their level of training. We're a mercenary ship. You've seen us do boardings before, but sometimes things don't go well and the boarders need help, or we get boarded. Or crap just happens at a station or dirtside. I make everyone practice so we don't die like sheep at a slaughterhouse." There I go with sheep again. Maybe I'm just feeling too vulnerable dirtside and the Bootlegger far away and my subconscious is playing with me.

"That's not exactly what I meant. It's the having to kill someone. How do you prepare for that part?"

"You don't kid." Nate answers with is eyes closed. Apparently he isn't fast asleep yet. "You do what you gotta do. Most of the time it comes down to either you or them. Killing ain't easy on your soul. That first kill, either you get beyond it, or you don't. Sometimes your kill is nothing more than selfishness that you want to live and he's gotta die to do it."

Time for me to chime in. "We're mercenaries and smugglers. Killing comes with the job. Giving the order to fire on an enemy ship really isn't any different than pulling the trigger on a gun on a man. I'm making a conscious decision to potentially end the life of another human being. Only the scale changes. While I don't relish those decisions, and I know a few real pirates that do, it's a part of the life we've chosen to live as free people away from the reaches of the Unitary Nations of EarthSpace or Confederated Colonies. There's a lot of gray area in the life and death decisions we face, but all we can do is follow our personal code and conscience as best as we can. "

"I guess when it happens it happens and I just have to deal with it."

"Short form yes. Less short, try to follow your conscience, which I assume since you're asking you have one, as best as you can in the conditions presented to you. Sometimes your standards may even slip. If they do then you cope with that as best as you can too. They slip beyond the point of what I permit on-board the ship and then I going to act within my conscience and take action. Now, as we're gonna be here for a bit longer and I'm just as tired as Chief Nate there, I'm gonna take a nap. I don't look as bad as he does only because I use better makeup than the chief does to cover the dark circles under my eyes, "

Nate starts grumbling about the makeup comment and how he can't wait until our next martial arts practice to show me dark circles under eyes or something and starts to nod off into dreamland as do I.

***

"Midshipman Pritchard! You're about to board a pirate ship, and look at the state of your weapon! Your rifle magazine is half out and your safety is off! You're leading the third section! Lock and load and get your act together! Your men are depending on you to look and act like an officer!" the first officer of the Bainbridge hollers at me. God this is nerve racking! He's right though. Get your ass in gear girl and stop the Nervous Nelly crap. You've drilled shipboard actions before, this isn't any different. Well, except for the real bullets and possible death part. Okay I key on the safety, tap my magazine to get it properly seated and pull the charging handle to get her loaded and ready. I tighten my helmet just a bit more as it keeps slipping down from all the sweat under it and walk out in front of the men in my section of the boarding party. We're just supposed to be a backup to the two other parties leading the boarding action but that doesn't mean we won't see action if someone gets past the first two teams or they meet heavy resistance. Oh God, did I pee before I came here? It would seriously suck to have to go while on the pirate ship...I don't want to imagine what their head looks like... Ewww nasty...Stop it, you're getting distracted. Ok, here are the men.

"Sergeant, is the third section rrready?" Damn my voice is cracking a bit as I address the leading non-com.

"Marines ready and waiting sir!" Sergeant...? Okamba? I don't remember already. Yes Okamba, right on his left breast pocket, duh.

"Very good, Sergeant." I turn to address the men in general and shoulder up my rifle. "Okay boys listen up, we're the backup section for this boarding." A few groans and whines... "we are to secure the backsides of sections one and two as they make the sweeps aboard the pirate ship. You guys know the drill already. Uploaded into your tac-comps is the ship's deck layout as this class is normally designed back at its shipyard. I shouldn't have to mention it but I will for your sleepy types" finally getting my groove here, "WHO ARE NOT PAYING ATTENTION!" as I kick the shins of some new marine to get his attention. "Thank you. As I was saying, you have the normal deck layout schematics but being a pirate vessel they probably modified it but we don't know how extensively. So keep your auto-mapping on and running. No less than four people at any given time without explicit orders from the Sergeant or myself. I catch anybody wandering off looking for pirate booty is going to get my boot in their booty." Did I just say that? Wow, that's just lame.

We file into the pirate ship after the 2nd section and just a short ways down we open right up into what seems to be the ship's mess hall. We take some positions here, as there are few ways into the mess hall and it's the only way back to the hallway that passes back to the Bainbridge. It doesn't take long for the shooting to start. Automatic weapons fire is going on down the hallways.

Braapp! Brapp!! Boom! Boom!

Grenades? Those sound a lot louder than grenades going off! What the hell?

"Auto seals activating due to decompression." I hear a mechanical voice say aloud over speakers.

"Ms. Pritchard! Ms. Pritchard!" Someone yells over the tac-comp's comms-net. "The airseal between the Bainbridge and us has been blown away! Sir, we're cut off! Do you hear me? Ms. Pritchard!?"

***

"Ms. Pritchard! Captain Pritchard!" I awake to Governor Edgerton waking me up in a hurry.

BOOM! BOOM!

More explosions are going off around me. This isn't my dream.

"What the heck is going on?! What's those explosions?" I start asking loudly as I'm waking up. It's just past dusk and I can see flashes and further off explosions through the windows of the room.

"We're being attacked! I don't know who but there are some sort of military forces attacking various points in the city. The city center is being run over as we speak. We need to move to a more secure location." Kyle explains as he is motioning to the door. We can meet up with my aide in my private office. From there we can use the back stairs to get to the ground cars and get out of here."

"Marlene, the buildings internal comms are down and so are our personal comms to the Bootlegger's net. They're jamming us." Nate mentions as he's been banging away at a terminal trying to call up anybody. I see Danny's been fiddling with his personal comm trying to get some signal from the Bootlegger, and here I am still clearing away the fog from my brain.

"Governor, have you got an extra-planetary capable transmitter somewhere nearby? Something strong enough that can reach high orbit ships or the asteroid colonies in system? I have the Bootlegger on planet near the ocean refueling reaction mass. A transmitter that strong may be able to punch though this interference and if we can hook it up into our comms-net, I can get the Bootlegger over here. She's got electronic protection measures against this kind of jamming and both her and our fighters can provide air cover.

"It's in this building! There's a terminal near my back stairs exit for the town's original planetary transmitter. It's along the same route we'd leave the building with but the access codes are in my office standalone computer. We have to stop there first. Most people have forgotten about it once the space port one was installed. This way." as he leads us out into the hall.

First Kill

***

We manage to take a set of stairs that avoided any hard contact encounters but we did see some men in tactical gear moving around on some of the floors on our way up to the Kyle's office. Kyle produced a handgun on his person and was even wearing a form fitted 'bullet-proof vest'. Should stop a handgun sized round but any rifle shot from the attackers is gonna go thru like it was a sheet of paper. Better than the frag all nothing we're wearing. We've made almost to the Governor's office when Nate motions us to stop and hold position. I move up slowly to his point position.

"Ok Chief, what's got you spooked?"

"I hear movement. Someone's in there but I hear some voices and they don't sound like friendlies."

"How sure are you?"

"Sure enough that I'd definitely 'frag and clear' if I had a grenade."

"I suppose by that remark you didn't pack any?"

"Hey, this IS supposed to be a friendly place."

"But you brought the rifle?"

"Was planning on getting a little hunting in."

"Alright, here's how were gonna play it. Lets back up a bit first before they hear us." as I back us away from the door a few meters.

"Mr. Garrett please be so kind to go to the bathroom back there and find me a bar of soap or something about that sized."

"Aye, aye Captain." as Danny quietly moves off to the bathroom.

"Ok, Kyle, you're gonna open the door and pull it back with you behind it all the way then take up position behind Chief Nate looking for targets of opportunity. Nate you take top and targets further back, Danny and I will take left and right front targets. If there's a heavy, take him wherever he is. Ah, Danny good, you're with me to my left and low, just as we've practiced on ship. When the door opens wait a fraction of a second after I go before you guys move into the doorway. Everyone clear? Good."

Everyone takes up positions as I ready the bar of soap. "Kyle, now!" Kyle pulls open the door and just before I get into position I toss the bar of soap into the room. "Fire in the hole!!" I holler into the room for effect. Of course its just a bar of soap not a grenade so instead of pulling back as if an explosion was about to go off, I drop to a knee and start shooting, while Danny and Nate take up positions and start firing. Three men go scattering away from my improvised grenade just long enough to let us get the first shots in. Three men go down right away. I plug two easy and Nate gets one further back closer to the Governor's desk.

"Clear?" I ask to no one in particular.

"Looks clear. Lets move up slowly Captain." Nate warns cautiously.

"Aye aye, Chief." I respond. Could still be someo...

Bang! Brrapp!! Bang! Bang!

"I got him Captain! I got him!" Danny starts up excitedly. "He was hiding behind the desk and he just popped up and I shot him!" The guy nearly hosed us with his rifle but thankfully he went wide.

"Good work Danny. Everyone, secure this room now." I order

and wipe my brow when no one looks.

We move through the room and find no other surprises other than the Governor's aide, already dead behind the desk on the floor.

"No! Rufus! No!" Kyle rushes over to his aide's lifeless body to hold him. "He was no soldier, just a good and decent man. "

"Sorry about your aide Kyle, but we have to move. Where are those codes?"

"The computer right there." He points out through the tears on his face to a older fashioned terminal on the corner of his desk. "It looks like it's locked down with Rufus codes. He was trying to lock down this machine to keep people out of it." He types up a few things and the screen unlocks. "I've got the codes printing now. Should come up over there. " he points to a printer to his right near Danny.

"Danny, grab that printout will you. Danny? Danny?" I walk over to Danny and see him staring at the person he just shot. I look over and see the man he just killed. His head is mostly gone. Danny managed to put two of his bullets into this poor guy's head and it just exploded like a overripe cantaloupe. There is blood and brain gore splattered all over the printer and wall.

"He's the first man I ever killed, and look at him. He has almost no head." Danny comments in a strangely quiet voice.

"Good, Danny, it means he went out fast and didn't even feel anything."

Nate says aloud as he's checking the bodies of the other soldiers. "Captain, I'm sure these were Unitaries. Why did they even bother to pretend to not be? Who else is going to be packing M-221 rifles except Unitary Nations EarthSpace Marines? I mean they're bio-locked so only the soldier it was issued to can normally use it, they use a odd-ball ammo cartridge, and if he dies it permanently disables itself so no one else can use pick it up off a battlefield and use it with out striping it down and cleaning it. Always hated that system. Damned things for no reason think you died in the middle of combat. There's other standard spec ops type gear as well here. Why the black ops? They aren't fooling anyone."

"It's probably for the eventual news reports." Chimes up Kyle with tears streaked on his face. "Back 'home', they don't think there's any real fighting going on. Just some outlaws making a ruckus. What I don't get is why us? We're a really small colony and technically unaligned because of it. We're just three settlements on this planet and we mostly make foodstuffs. I don't get it."

"We can think about all this later. Danny. Danny! Snap out of it." I order him as I'm shaking him to get his to focus. "We need to go. Grab those printouts and lets get the hell out of here." Danny grabs the printouts just in time as he vomits all over the printer. This isn't going to be good.

***

We managed to take the vests off of the four dead men. They are much better than what Kyle was wearing. Might have half a chance against a rifle round now. We took their ammo on the off chance we find a few Unitary soldiers that are wounded but not dead. Nate knows how to bypass the bio-lockout on one of their rifles, but it takes a bit of time and fiddling to do it. We head to the stairs in Kyle's private office and head down a few floors to the first sub-basement level. Kyle assures us that this is the way to the transmitter and our eventual exit. He leads us into a room just off the hallway that leads further towards the garage. It's unmarked and looks like a janitor's main storage room. In the back, Kyle moves a few boxes and reveals a small desk and terminal.

"Always meant to get a remote access extension to this system from my office, but Rufus always kept pointing out there was more important things to spend our colony's resources on." He starts flipping switches and banging away on the keyboard bringing the thing to life. "This is gonna take a few minutes." he tells us.

"Nate, you and Danny go back into the hall and cover the ends, so we don't get surprised by anyone."

"Danny, lets move." Nate orders. Technically Danny's a ship officer but as a midshipman and still essentially a trainee, and Nate being a senior non-commissioned officer, Nate's in charge. Danny is still in a fog. He locks up on us at the wrong moment and someone could pay the price for it. This just isn't a good time for this. But then again there never really is a good time to kill people, I suppose. Any EarthSpace soldiers find us here and we'll be pinned down badly. That reminds me of my first real fire fight. Being pinned down really sucks.

***

"Ms. Pritchard. This is Lieutenant Lucas. We're pinned down badly and section two is gone. These aren't your typical pirates. They are much better organized. They bloody well planned and prepared for defending against a boarding operation. You need to take your section to Engineering and get control of this ship. They fix their fold engines and fold away and we are screwed hard. It isn't going to be easy but you're the only mobile and functional section we have." Oh crap. This has just gone from bad to worse. Trapped on a pirate ship and no way to call, let alone get reinforcements. The Bainbridge won't shoot at us now, with us on board. Well, I hope not. If they get their fold engines back online they could leave with us on board. We were lucky to disable them the first time around! Now Miss Greenhorn and her merry band of Marines have to fight their way to engineering so we can have any chance of living thru this cluster-mess.

"Ok boys, listen up! New game plan. We just got moved to point. Section one is pinned down and section two has been blown to hell and gone. Comms to the Bainbridge are jammed and just for the icing on the cake, these guys may get their fold engines back on line, leaving us in all sorts of a bad situation. Okamba, get these men to move out."

"Ok you heard the officer, move out people! Randall, you're on point." Okamba stars barking orders as we move out.

We get all of one minute out and Randall shouts back to us, "Take cover!"

Well crap. That didn't take us long to run into trouble. They set up for us at the third junction in the hallway just as we make a left turn towards Engineering. Suddenly, I see two of my men dash to cover in an intersection with two hatchways in front of me, and beyond them I see several pirates shooting at us. While everyone else piles back around the corner into the passageway we were coming up from, I dive to the floor and roll to the right hatchway with Private Randall.

"Sir you're hurt." Huh? Oh hell, he's right. I'm bleeding from my nose as I somehow managed to land on my face. So much for looking like a dignified officer.

"Don't worry about it, shoot! Shoot!" I peek around the hatch combing that they have five people that can shoot at us compared to five of us, but they're fifty meters back and set up one high and one low on both sides of the passageway, and the fifth is on the deck laying flat. On our side of the hallway, three of us are trapped behind hatch combing, and the rest are behind us back at the corner we came from, but back there only two of my men can get a gun around the corner at one time, one high and one low. Tactically, we suck.

"Ahoogh!"

Just lost the man across from us in the other hatchway. He stuck himself out too far.

This is probably a bad idea, "Private, stay here and keep shooting, I'm going across." as I dash across the intersection to the other hatchway and I before I can start shooting my tac-comp chirps.

First Kill

"Okamba to Prichard, what's the situation sir?"

"They have five guys in front of us and we only have four shooters, including me. You have two of them with you on the corner behind us! What the hell do you think?! We're pinned down here with bad cover!"

"I can see. What can I do?"

"What can you do?!? GET more MEN in the hallway! Get me a grenade down that hallway!"

"We don't have anything except flash-screamers and smoke." Mental note to self, I should start carrying some concussion grenades.

"Well keep shooting and use a smoke to get some more men in the hallway."

Okay girl, I guess this is real combat. Did I just pee my pants? Ok, get a good grip on this rifle, get down and first target! Breathe!! Pause!

Bang!

Head shot! Whoa – back up! They are emptying magazines like its going out of style or something. Okay again, look! Breath, pause.

Bang!

Got the center guy this time! That's two down. There's the smoke finally. Sounds like there's three more guys coming up from the back hall now.

Brrap! Brap! Bang! Bang!....

Am I the only one that paid attention in rifleman class?? Placed shots work better than hosing the place down. Dammit it's too loud! I can't cover my ears and shoot at the same time! The noise right next to me!

"Clear! Clear!" I start to hear as the shots stop firing.

I get up and can see that several of the men are now with Okamba down the hallway where the shooters were. Someone hands me a compress for my nose.

"Nice shots there sir!" Private Randall starts to tell me. "Two head-shots and looks like you got a third on the right side as well! And all by yourself!"

I move up and look at the two dead half headless men...and I puke over the third man. I can't believe I just threw up on a dead man... One I just killed, no less... My God the blood is everywhere... What did I just do?

Looking up towards Sergeant Okamba, I muster up some courage. "Okay, lets keep moving boys. Okamba, form them back up." I order as it's my job to lead these men. Just as killing those men was my job.

"I'm sorry you had to die." I mutter under my breath at the dead men.

***

As I see the Chief coming back from the garage I snap myself out of my reverie. "Nate, how's Midshipman Garrett?" I ask my senior non-comm as he comes back to the small utility closet that holds the comm terminal.

"Not good, he's not focused and sort of keeps brooding. If we we're out of action it wouldn't be a problem and we could help him through it but right now, he might get himself or us killed. I came back to tell you that I managed to jam the door the way we came in and the other on the branching hallway. Keep an ear out for any breaking noises back that way. Now this way I can keep my eyes on the garage and Danny for a while."

"Good thinking. Get going, I'll stay in the doorway." I tell Nate as he walks off towards the garage.

"How are we coming Governor?"

"I have the system up and waiting for a signal. I think there's a problem with the antenna array. I can't tell what the problem is from here. The antenna is actually on the building next to us across the courtyard. There is a hard-line buried between us."

"Can you set up a repeating message from here based off my codes to do a general broadcast while we go look at the antenna?"

"Easily."

"Okay. Set up a message asking for help using my codes for our comm-net, and I'll include a codeword for my first officer to recognize. Then we go outside and to the other building to find the antenna array and try to fix it."

***

Kyle sets up the message and we make our way outside though the garage. Plans change when in contact with the enemy as we didn't take a gravcar. Not really needed to get though the courtyard between the buildings. Taking a look around outside, I see smoke and various signs of combat all over. Not total devastation but you can tell there's been some fighting at the street level here. I still don't get it. Why hit this colony? They don't have any weapons except for personal stuff. Plenty of that, but so does every other colony. It's not like they are supplying ship armaments or anything like that. They produce foodstuffs. Mostly outlying farms and some processing and packaging factories. The Governor takes us towards the building with the antenna.

"Ah crap! Here's the problem." he cries out. I see a small crater and body parts from some dead colonists ringing the crater. I'm guessing the hole was made by some small man sized mortar or larger rocket grenade but I don't know what he's referring to. "Right here. See this cable?" as he holds up a partial section of cable coming out of the ground. "You can guess where this leads back to." The remaining ends are over 3 meters apart. It's a specialized cable so we can't just stick any old wire between them.

"CONTACT! TAKE COVER!!" Nate yells as were being fired upon! We all dive into the crater that's now become a shallow foxhole.

"Where's the hard contact Nate??" I ask. The gunfire sounds like its everywhere.

"To the north between the buildings across the compound. I see... ten, no make it sixteen people, maybe more. Looks like a squad … roughly."

"We can go south and get behind the buildings and get away but we're gonna take fire doing so."

"We're eventually toast here." Pipes up Kyle. "It's about a ten meter dash. I say lets go!"

"Yeah, let move it. Danny! Let's move!" But Danny is already out of the crater hole and moving south to get around the building cover.

"Ahhh hell!! GO! GO! GO!"

Danny seems to make it as I'm barely halfway. I'm not exactly a world class sprinter but with someone shooting at you, you learn to move fast. I hear automatic gunshots being fired as I run, coming from behind us and wait for the inevitable zing of a near misses or pain of a hit but somehow I make it to cover with Nate safely.

"Capt, they ain't shooting at us." Danny peers around the corner. "Look."

I take his spot peering around the corner and see that they are firing roughly 90 degrees to our left. I trace their line of fire towards various gravcars and buildings and see the local colonists fighting back! They seem to outnumber the soldiers almost two to one! "Nate take a look at this! The colonists are fighting back!"

"Heh, what you expect with these folks? Lemme see. Sure as space is black, they are fighting back hard but they're disorganized. The soldiers are concentrating their fire at larger groups forcing them down while someone else shoots away at a colonist who thinks he's safe to poke his head out. Those colonists need to organize and coordinate their own fire or the solders are gonna make salsa out of them."

"That's why we're trying to get the Bootlegger over here with her EPM gear to cut the static and coordinate all of these guys. Although at this rate, it's gonna be a while."

"Marlene, these guys don't have that long. Hell, all of us here don't have that long. Just look at them right now! We won't stand a chance in a protracted combat!" cries Kyle as he's looking at a small sample of the disaster that's already befallen this settlement.

"Dammit I know!" He's right, the colonists were sucker punched and with all the chaos most of the settlement is going to be dead from just a few squads of Unitary Army grunts.

"Alright. Chief, I've got an idea. You and the Governor work your way to those colonists over there and help them organize and try to make that group a cohesive force and then expand from them as best as you can. Danny and I are going to the landing field and see if we can get to our shuttle. We'll take off and head out towards the Bootlegger. We should be able to reach the Bootlegger on comms once we're clear of the jamming zone."

"Great, except they are probably watching the landing zone for anyone trying to get away and get help from one of the other nearby settlements." Trust Chief Nate to point out the sticky part of my plans. Not really much choice. A gravcar would also work, but would be slower and a much easier target going out of the settlement. Besides if they were smart they'd have mined the roads and pathways going out of the settlement to keep everyone contained. They might blow up the landing field, but I have a feeling their exfiltration shuttles are going to land there to pick the soldiers up otherwise they would have to make their way though the forests around most of this settlement.

"I don't see to many other ways to play this? Do you?"

"Nope just pointing out the sticky parts of the plan." I smile as he says that.

"You guys get moving then. We'll see you in a few hours." I hope.

They move off towards the fighting colonists leaving me and Danny behind.

"You good, Danny?"

"Honestly, no, but I'm functional. I won't let you down Captain."

"Good. Lets get moving."

It took us a good half hour to walk cautiously to the landing field, but I was trying to be extra careful. The last thing I wanted is for us to be jumped and...

First Kill

CRACK!

"Owww! What the..."

...and everything goes black.

***

Surprisingly, we haven't run into any further resistance along our way towards engineering. It's fine by me if Lady Luck wants to smile on us, I'm not the kind of girl to argue good fortune. On the tac-comp I can see section one's position and the location of probable enemies. We had to plot around to the opposite side of their position to get into engineering section of this ship. We're about to enter engineering when one of the point men halts the section.

"Okamba, what's the score?" I ask my leading non-comm as I move up to him and the point man.

"Well sir, looking at the map and from the last feeds from section one, normal combat doctrine states that we go in with smoke grenades or flash-screamers and hit them hard. But because they're hiding in covered positions slightly further down, the flash-screamers may not be as effective. Also with them being further away in cover than is doctrinally ideal, we can't hit them as hard so we'll need to use up more men right away in ..."

Did he memorize the EarthSpace Marine tactical rule book or something? He must be bucking for a promotion to officer.

"...thereby if we go with using smoke, that will help us get in fast and get to cover positions but then we'll just be stuck in a slugging match while they continue to fix the fold-drive systems. It's statistically hard to ..."

I interrupt him and hold up my hand to his face. "Hold on, short form, we either go in fast and get shot up or go in slower and don't get so shot up but risk losing the ship outright and getting separated permanently from the Bainbridge. Recommendations?"

"As I was saying sir, I don't know." he sort of flusters to me. Now I know he's bucking for officer, he's learned to not make decisions that might bite him in the butt later on. "We are ordered to take engineering to prevent them from getting the fold system going and that obviously has a time restriction on our tactical plan. But if we get all shot up trying to take them we're really in no better of a spot if the men do get there fast enough."

In other words, my call. He doesn't want to get blamed for making the wrong suggestion if this goes badly. Sigh..why can't anyone just be straight up in this Space Navy? If this goes badly, I'm the one in charge here, not him. There has got to be a way to do this quickly and with out killing most of my men, not to mention myself. "Sarge, get me a fiber-cam around the corner quickly please." I need to get a real look at the situation myself. A grunt comes up from the back and runs a fiber-optic camera cable around the corner and a picture comes up on my tac-comp screen.

"Sarge, look at the vid feed. Tell me, those big tanks, look like the ships reaction mass tanks?"

"And doesn't that look like the control system panel right about where one of our cover positions would be?" I point out one of the cover positions we'd use.

"It looks like it. Why?"

"Sergeant, set up for smoke, we're going in to the cover positions. Starting there."

Water's been used as a reaction mass for ship drive systems ever since the High Output Fusion Plasma drive was developed for sub-luminal space travel. It's easy to store and plentiful on Earth, and later discovered habitable planets once the space fold system was developed. If planet-side water isn't available, any icy comets out there can be used to melt some from or other material can be used these days as well. Some environmental groups on Earth got the military and commercial ships in Earth Space to use crushed rock from asteroids versus water, as they were worried about the environmental impact of losing some fractionally infinitesimal amount of water from habitable planets. But water is by far the easiest to get and use. Once fold technology was developed that water found another use. By spraying a bubble around the ship of water the fold system's energy field can be tightly defined and controlled within the sphere of water or ice crystals. So space folding always uses a bunch of water sprayed out various ports to enable a ship to fold space. Many times a smaller ship can ride shotgun on a larger ship's fold cloud and even some battle formations are coordinated using a really large cloud and well timed fold engines.

The way I see it, we can disable the fold system even if they get it working. And even keep this ship from maneuvering away as well, giving the Bainbridge time to get reconnected to this ship. All we have to do is dump out their water tanks using the controls on the water tank's station. This won't be easy as I have to have my boys maneuver through the smoke and help cover my position at the control panel. That assumes they don't figure out what were doing before its too late. Maybe Mom was right and I should have gone to law school.

Deep breath - "Okay men, we're not going try to take engineering. We're going to take over that position one on your maps, as well as fight from right around here. Okamba and I are going to empty those tanks out."

"We are?" Suddenly he looks like a frightened animal.

"Yes we are. It's a forward position and only under partial cover. I'm not asking anyone else to do something I'm not willing to do." Even though unofficial Unitary military doctrine says let the lowest men in the ranks do the dirty work. "We empty those tanks, and this ship doesn't move in local space and it can't fold away from the

Bainbridge with us stuck on it."

I start directing a few of my Marines to where they are going to go and get ready for us to make our run. I estimate the number of steps that it will take me to cover the distance to the reaction mass tank control system so I can do it under smoke cover and bullet fire.

"Ready? Go!" I rush off to the control panel, Okamba right on my heels.

I can hear weapons fire through the smoke and a even see a few zings forming contrails in the smoke. It's so loud it's drowning out the machinery sounds all around, and my hearing dampers are on constantly. Lets see, I'm blind, deaf and definitely dumb.

I slide into the control panel, and to relative safety behind its bulk of steel paneling and machinery but I don't see Okamba behind me.

"Okamba! Report!" Nothing. "Okamba!" Still nothing. Then I remember the squad readout on my tac-comp on my sleeve. I punch commands to check Okamba's life signs and I get a flat line.

I flatten myself on the control panel as best as I can with my rifle stuck out far to my left, shooting blindly while I use my right hand to manipulate the control panel to vent the tanks completely. Alright! The tanks are dumping into space! But this is just the manual control system, I need to also manage to keep the computer control from engineering or the bridge from overriding the controls on this station. Crap, how the hell do I do this one handed? Gunfire is everywhere around my head. I can barely think! I need to disable the computer interface here quickly! How? How? How? Suddenly it hits me and I pull out my combat knife from my back and just stab the computer terminal a few times. Sparks fly and I take a zap of electricity but the computer interface to the tank control panel seems dead and the valves are open. Yea! Go team good guys! We did it!

First Kill

CRACK!

Owww, what the...

Everything goes black.

***

"Captain! Thank God you're alright! You blacked out on me for a minute!"

"I'm not so sure about the 'alright' Danny. Oww. Got me between my gut and my right lung. Might have hit the lung, it's a little hard to breathe." So much for the better body armor. "Sit-rep, Danny. I need to know the score."

"Shooter got you from the rooftop. I managed to shoot back and quickly drag you to cover, but he's still got the drop on us, he saw where we went."

"Where are we?"

"In a small shop across from the landing field area. Seems two settlers made a stand here recently and died. They left behind a hunting rifle with some ammo. Got a nice scope on it but only five rounds left."

"These windows face towards our shooter?" As I point to the shot out windows on the wall facing the street where I assume we came in from.

"Yes."

"And that's our only door as well?"

"Yes, ma'am." he dejectedly replies.

"Help me look."

"Uh..that's probably not a good idea Captain, he knows where we are."

"True, but I need to see the situation." Learned a long time ago to see a tactical situation for yourself if you like living.

"Alright, hold on to me, Captain." Danny lifts me up and over towards the window. "I see him. Whoa!" A shot hits the window frame just a bit to my right of my face!

"Okay, bad idea, but I have a better one. Take that rifle, Danny, and set up towards the back of the room over by the other windows. But go around the room so he doesn't see you. You should be in relative darkness over there and it will be harder for him to see you from his position. I'm going to stick this lady's head up in this window. You scan where the shooter is and take him out."

"This gonna work, Captain?" Danny asks me with a incredulous look on his face.

"Sure it will. He will take a shot towards me, giving you just enough time to get a line on him."

"But that woman..."

"She's dead. She won't mind." I interrupted him. "I don't like desecrating a body either but we're in this for our lives Danny."

"I mean, how are you gonna lift her? You can barely lift yourself!"

"Oh. Good point. Help me get her in position. I can lift her up the last bit. Gonna hurt like hell though."

Danny drags the girl, we determined, of maybe late teens or

potentially early twenties, over to the window and prop her up so I can push her up my myself. Oww, this still hurts. I'm bleeding but not gushing. No major artery hit. Thank God for small favors.

"Danny hold a sec. Take off her jacket and tie it around my torso." Not the best bandage but it will do. "Okay, thats good. Get into position." Danny heads towards the back and slides on the floor like a snake.

"I'm ready Captain."

"Okay here I go." I grunt and push hard trying to lift this body up so her head sticks out. Oh good GOD!! THE PAIN!! Our shooter takes the bait and shoots at the head. Danny is lying on the floor with the rifle aimed out the window. He breathes, pauses, shoots five times in perfect cadence. He's been practicing his rifleman skills as well, I see. Good. No hesitation on his part.

"He's down, Captain."

"Are you sure?"

"Yes I am. The spray from his head looked like the guy I shot with my pistol back at the city center, except messier. I saw half his head go." His voice is kind rough as he says that. He's trying to be brave and not scared and he seems to be holding it barely together, but holding it.

"Excellent shooting form there. I see you've been practicing your rifle skills as well. I estimate that was 250 meters with a head-shot."

"Would have been all five if he didn't go down with the first shot. I shouldn't have fired the rest, but I wasn't thinking just trying to shoot at the same spot." He says matter-of-factually. Not bragging, just stating the facts like he was discussing the weather dirt-side or something. It's a bit disconcerting.

"It was just fine. Help me up here and lets get going. I'm gonna have to lean on you to walk."

"Aye aye, Captain."

***

We get moving again but it only takes us ten minutes to see a new problem. Once we get to the open landing field proper, we see a man moving around the hatchway of our shuttle. Assuming that their electronic comms jamming will probably affect them due to the saturation nature of the jamming, he probably doesn't know one of his lookouts is dead. Knowing that they know they don't have regular comms available they must have some way of checking in regularly. Either he leaves or the sniper leaves his position and gets in sight of the shuttle to check in visually. That gives us a small window of opportunity here to work with. Getting smaller as I'm getting weaker. I'm coughing up some blood now. I guess if I didn't hit the lung before I must have tore something while moving the girl.

"Danny, put me down." I really didn't notice but he's practically been carrying me at this point. We're behind some crates a few dozen meters away from our shuttle. "There's someone in the shuttle and it's definitely not a colonist. We only have a short amount of time at best until someone notices the dead guy we left behind. I can't take him. I can't even..."

"I got this one." He interrupts me. "I need to kill him, and fast, then come back for you. I understand what I need to do. " He's very calm and collected now. I hope he's alright.

"You okay?"

"No. I'm not. But that's part of it isn't it? I don't want to be okay having to kill someone. I..I don't ever want to be the kind of man where it's that easy. I understand now. You do what you have to do but always keep that internal moral compass aligned with your beliefs. It's necessary however for him to die. I'm sorry he has to die so we can live but that's the essence of it. I want to live and I believe that helping these colonists is the right thing to do. I can't persuade him to give up our shuttle while he shoots me, and I can't help the colonists if we're dead. So I'll kill him before he kills me."

I wasn't expecting that from him. I think he just aged 10 years right before my eyes. That schoolboy looks of his is just gone. Maybe he was better off the way he was before. Who am I to rip his innocence away? His captain.

"Here take my rig. The extra guns and ammo won't hurt." I start to unstrap my gunbelt and holsters and find I'm having a hard time doing it. "A little help here?" Danny reaches around me and takes my belt and fits it to himself, just barely. He reminds me of Chief Nate. A younger, blonder version, but between his shoulder-holstered gun and now two on his thighs and the extra ammo magazine pouches in-between, he's now the walking armory.

"I'll be right back, Captain." He walks stealthily off towards our shuttle. I'm leaning up against the crates and I'm too weak to maneuver myself around the corner to see. Dammit all anyhow!

Pistol fire goes off. I can't count the shots but there are plenty. The first set is definitely .45s from my Colt. The answering fire is definitely not mine or Danny's. It's automatic rapid fire. Sounds like a sub-gun. Makes sense. It would be a lot easier to handle in close confines of the shuttle. The gunfire stopped. I don't hear anything. Did the guy in the shuttle kill Danny? Should I call out to Danny to see if he's alive? If he's dead then so am I. Maybe that's alright then. I was his Captain and I got him killed. I was supposed to keep him alive. "Please God, don't let me have sent another one off to die! Not him. Not now." I pray out loud.

"Huh? Only one dead is the ground pounder in the shuttle. He started coming out the hatchway as I approached. He was dead before he hit the ground. When he went down I think his finger jammed on the trigger and emptied his mag. I wasn't sure at the time, so I kept shooting him on the ground until he stopped. It's a bit messy at the entrance to the shuttle, sorry 'bout that." He sort of chuckles like it was a lame joke but neither of us are in the mood. He picks me up again and takes to the shuttle. He drops me off in a seat and starts to grab a med kit to help me.

"No Danny, get us out of here first. Get us up and out of the combat zone then you can help me. There's no bullet lodged inside me and I'm not gushing blood. While it hurts and I'm weak, I'll survive long enough to get back home. I might pass out for a bit though. Don't let me pass out for long if I do go out...

***

"Miss Pritchard. Hello? Marlene, you there? Hello! Gold Bricker. Trying to fake it huh?" I hear fuzzily from in front of my face. Its Eric and Jason, the two other midshipman on the Bainbridge. They're younger than me by a little but they're almost 20. Still more like 13 maturity wise, but they're decent guys.

"Where am I?" I've got a bandage around my gut but it doesn't hurt that bad. I feel kinda woozy as I try to sit up. There's the pain! Bad idea. I'll just lie down here on the bed for a while.

"Hold up there, missy. You've got a gut shot wound there. You don't want to be moving those muscles for a while now." Eric advises. Good advice. A bit late, but good advice.

"You're a hero. You saved the situation on the pirate ship." Jason starts up. "Brilliant idea going for the reaction mass tanks. Once those were emptied the Freebird was stuck on a single vector and it was easy for the Bainbridge to catch her and get a docking collar reattached. You didn't have to fight your way further into the engineering section, yet you still got those fold-drives inoperable. Absolutely brilliant! The Captain is putting you up for a commendation and says you're ready for your commission, Sub-Lieutenant." he says as he winks at me.

"Is what he saying true, Eric?" I ask. I'm still too foggy to believe it.

"Yup its true, Sub-Lieutenant. The Captain will probably be down later today after you've been awake and coherent for a bit. You're still pretty doped up on pain meds." Really? The pain in my gut doesn't agree .

"Thanks guys. How's the rest of my section from the boarding party?"

"Your Sergeant, what's his name .. Okamba." Heh, Jason couldn't remember it either. "He's dead. Neck shot, apparently following you. His spine was shot out." Not sure he exactly had one to start. Shame on me. He's dead. He followed his orders even as it killed him. "That could have easily been you. As for the rest of your squad, you lost four men, by far the least considering the second section was wiped out to the man and first section came back with only three men including Lieutenant Lucas, but he's injured badly. Explosive trap. Command will probably will rotate back home to a desk side job after a long hospital stay."

"You on the other hand, while gut shot, will heal up as the round passed right through you and didn't hit much that the Doc couldn't fix up here. You'll be bedside for a while and then on light duty, but you'll be back to normal with a few cool scars to show for it. You can show us later after you're all healed up." Eric leers. Boys.

"Don't hold your breath for that. I need some rest now so if you don't mind I'm gonna take a nap now, so as my first unofficial order as a commissioned naval officer, get out."

"Yes, sir! Sweet dreams." They both chime.

***

I'm starting to get really tired of gut shot wounds. My gut aches when I come-to in the shuttle. Used to be a gut shot wound was a slow and painful way to die, but with modern medicine it's now a slow and painful way to recover. Danny's gotten us away from the settlement and and has already called in the Bootlegger. We've docked with the Bootlegger at some midpoint between settlement one and the ocean I assume. Danny's already field dressed my wound and I think given me a painkiller. My gut still hurts but the edge is off.

I still can't figure out why they were waiting in our shuttle at the landing field and not any of the nearly dozen others that were there. Ours was nothing special that made it stand out compared to the others. There were a few larger and better armed cargo freighters on the field that were better centrally located than ours. I'm tempted to say they were looking for us, but without anything else it's just conjecture at this point. My gut, no pun intended, is telling me that this wasn't random or targeted solely at the colony.

"Okay Captain, I know you don't want this but I'm insisting. We're putting you on a stretcher and carrying you into the med bay." That's Doctor Julia Woods, ship's head surgeon. Lost her license to practice in the EarthSpace worlds but who's checking in the back end of known space? She's good and that's what counts. She knows I don't like to show weakness in front of the crew.

"Julia, this is my third gut shot wound. You can carry me. I sure as heck ain't walking."

"Good. I'm also sticking a saline IV in you. Your heart rate is faster than I like."

"Well that's the line. I can't go around with a IV in my arm. How would I look?" The look on her face is priceless. "It clashes with my guns and holsters."

First Kill

"You're not wearing your guns and holsters. Just for that I'm reducing your pain killer dosage by 25%. You don't seem to need it."

"Thanks." I say to her dryly. I'm in no condition to verbally joust with her. "Julia, have someone send my compliments to Mr. Samuels, and tell him that I'd like him to meet me in the med bay as soon as he can get away from the bridge."

"I still have to clean and sew your new holes back up. If you want to talk to him that will mean a local vs knocking you out. Might hurt a bit"

"I've done enough nap time already, a local will be just fine."

***

Samuels has the Bootlegger almost to Settlement One, and has already launched the two standby fighters and sent a shuttle for the other pilots if they can round them up. We're a little less aerodynamic than the fighters and shuttles, so we're moving in the air slower than we could actually do if we were in the vacuum of space.

"Johnny, I'm assuming you've already been briefed by Mr. Garrett?"

"Yeah. Damned lucky to get here alive I'd say."

"More than that. They were Unitary forces but they weren't wearing any standard marking on their uniforms. They were more like an oversized black ops team. They still had Unitary gear. See the gear on the dead guy Danny took out in the shuttle? They had their pick of shuttles and freighters to wait in, but its as if they planned for us to get to the landing field. Doesn't make much sense to me what their tactics were unless they had compartmentalized information and were only told where and what to look out for, but not why. In any case that's for later. The Bootlegger should be able to cut through the jamming and start coordinating with the people down there. You can probably find where they are jamming from as well. They don't seem to have any air support, so once we're in control of the air we should be able to help root out any pockets of attackers. Keep a few fighters out looking for combat landing shuttles or the like. Someone's gonna come to pick them up soon. I'd like to capture them if at all possible. Someone in the know is probably in the pickup craft, whatever it is."

"How do you figure, Capt?"

"So he can take credit by being there when they get back without actually having to have been on planet as part of the attacking forces. Most officers don't mind risking subordinates necks to gather the credit for themselves."

"Glad I was never in the Unitary Armed Forces. "

Well you're in my Space Navy now. Get back to the bridge and go take care of business. Doc's not letting me out of here for a while. Guess you're still in command. But I'm not far, mind you." I give him the evil eye in jest. He's a trustworthy man or he wouldn't be my first officer.

"As ordered, Captain."

***

Ships log: 2211-03-03

It didn't take too long to get control of the situation on the ground once the Bootlegger and our fighters showed up. Once we could communicate with people on the ground to help direct tactics and the soldiers couldn't communicate, it was all over. Seems the colonists have had a emergency militia response plan should they ever be attacked, Chief Nate explained to me when he got back to the ship. They were organized to some extent and fought back much harder than the Unitary soldiers expected, due more to their stubbornness than their skill, in Nate's opinion. But the lack of regular drilling as a militia on tactics and marksmanship showed in the end. Without our help this settlement would have had a lot more dead. I think Governor Kyle is planning on recruiting for a small regular militia from the planet's settlers. I know he's planning on making overtures to the two other asteroid based colonies in system to form a small system-wide government, then petition to become part of the Confederacy. Between foodstuffs and the asteroid mining, they have resources to offer in return for some protection. We still need to get our food stores replenished so the Governor is going to make a stop to the Bootlegger for our negotiations. He's already hinted at making a donation of what we need as some sort of payback for helping the colony supplies.

Timothy and his gang of fighter jock reprobates found a inbound "freighter" that looked a bit more like a troop transport to him and managed to capture it. It's now down on the landing field with the Bootlegger while the other ship's captains have cleared off from the settlement, so between us and our prize we've been taking up all of the landing space, and then some. There was a officer in charge from afar on board, as I predicted. Between him and the soldiers we captured on the ground, it seems they were waiting for us after all. Or someone like us. It seems that someone in the EarthSpace government got wind of privateers coming to Farbrook colony to resupply, and somewhere along the line, it got turned into Farbrook was some sort of weapons resupply depot and that the colony is nothing more than a front for the Confederacy remote resupply. Maybe now it will be, but it wasn't before. They kept a small craft waiting for any ship to fold in, and when we came in we were just the kind of bait they were looking for. Apparently a secondary op was to capture the Governor and someone from the the ship that came in system so they could find out the details or our 'arms smuggling' arrangement. With the Bootlegger coming here for foodstuffs for a while now, and we are probably the most notable warship that comes by, that makes us somewhat responsible I figure. Well probably only me figures that, but I do feel guilty about what happened here. I'm going to have to spread out some of our resupply trading or just bite the bullet and use more of what the Confeds offer for non-weaponry items. Our Letter of Marque allows us to resupply from Confederate shipyards, but supplies are usually the not the best of the lot, but we get decent trade terms for it. They reserve the better gear and supplies for their small space navy first. Maybe with all the downtime I'm going to have in the next few weeks I can plot out a few new places to shop.

I'm planning on taking all the Unitary men with us and the troop transport. The Confeds will pay nicely for the transport, as well as the soldiers and the mid ranking officer who planned this operation and then ran it from far away. They will glean intel from them that helps them gain an edge on the United EarthSpace worlds in one way or another. I just want the armaments they'll provide me in exchange.

Mr. Garrett seems to have gotten a lot older in just a few days. Your first kill, or kills in his case, will do that. It's a hard moral quandary we live in as mercenaries but he's managed to find where his moral compass is and can stick to it with out beating himself up about it. It's a hard hump to get over, but he made it and I'm proud to have him on board. He's still young, at 18, for a full officer promotion, especially to 3rd officer of the ship, but he's been acting quartermaster for a while now that I think its time to make it official and to start rotating him into Chief Sann's armory as well. He's gonna make a fine officer one day.

As for me, well my injuries are healing mostly. My large intestine thankfully only got nicked but I'm on liquid and soft diets until it heals up. Guts shots are no fun but physically I'll recover. Mentally, I think I'm still trying to recover from my own first kills almost 15 years ago and every one since then.

I'm sorry all of you had to die.

Patrick A. Waldoch *is a Computer System-Network BOfH (look it up) with too many expensive hobbies. Between motorcycle track days (when he can scrounge up the cash for track fees), practical shooting sports (when he can scrounge up the cash for ammunition), and his girlfriend (when he can scrounge up the cash for dinners and sparkly things for her -- just kidding she's the best!), he also plays RPG's regularly with other authors from this volume. At Gencon you might know him as one of the dwarves from Bad Apple Inc,- Grumpy.*

A Pacifist March to War

Catalino Tolejano, II

Urzzt had long believed in the code. His progenitors didn't see it as something to live by; they saw it as folly in the face of all that the Imperium had accomplished. They'd rather he live and be a part of society than be an outcast or worse, a criminal. He knew there was paradox in his code, as was common with most beings' beliefs, but it was still something he knew to be the true calling of the Universe. The Movement was, in Urzzt's mind, a manifestation of Urzzt's code shared across several Worlds in the Imperium. This solidified his belief that he was on the righteous path, that of the true code which has been corrupted through the petty interactions of zealots clambering to be the most pure by destroying the foundation of the beliefs. In spite of that, Urzzt still knew he was right to stay with the Movement. He had a Destiny to fulfill! Of which he had no idea. Peace and Wisdom called to him.

Urzzt didn't know how the Movement had fallen on such difficult times, but it was clear that the Movement was dying. This death was truly a making of their own splintered beliefs, working against one another and wreaking havoc across the other 16 member systems of the Imperium. The Movement was, at its roots, a teaching of harmony, peace, compassion, and empathy toward others. The idea that this had become a scourge on society was completely ludicrous, but things had been getting worse and worse for the Movement and he often cursed his inaction at a higher level. He wasn't ambitious like the zealots bringing about their demise, but perhaps it was time for him to consider alternative courses of action.

Eleven Galactic Cycles (GC) ago they had fled the core systems and headed out across the galaxy. They had sought planetary systems where they could create a new colony, far from the Imperium and on a world with the suitable requirements. They sought a planet in a habitable zone, one which they could xenoform into a world where they could live far from the hatred and violence which had rained death and distrust upon all the Movement's followers. Had it really been so long? Eleven GC meant that Urzzt's home system's two populated planets, Ula and Fent'Ud'alu, had revolved around their central star Apenimum eleven times! The mind could be lost thinking about what may or may not have happened in such time.

The surviving followers of the Movement had obtained two Colony-Class Xenoform Mark 4 (CX-M4) relics, with which to make their way across the Galaxy. Many felt that their self-exile, generously granted by the Imperium, was not final-enough for the Powers. The Movement's authority believed that once the Powers had allowed their 'scourge' to flee, the only path left for them would be to have the magistrate forces chase them down and eradicate the Movement from the Galaxy once and for all. Lest they return someday to plague the Imperium by sowing the seeds of peace amongst the worlds again. *Ha,* thought Urzzt, *to plague the home Worlds with their "harmony talk," as many of the nonbelievers called it.* And the Movement authority had been right... now only one ship was left of the two. They were fortunate to have one ship still, he knew, and the code taught Urzzt to see the universal good in outcomes that were also tragic. *Maybe that was unfortunate*, he thought, *as our trials are far from over.* He knew their death toll still hadn't satisfied the Universe. *Ironic that we named the CX-M4 "The Herald" before leaving the Imperium.*

Urzzt and his fellow fallen had traveled far in terrible squalor, having allowed the other ship to die so that the majority of followers could live. It meant running this CX-M4 ship at its maximum capacity for habitats and liquid reclamation, which take their toll on the vessel and the beings aboard during such lengthy voyages. This voyage had taken them far, to a place where a once-habitable planet existed in an almost-ideal location for the colonization process, revolving around a yellow star as the fourth planet in the system. There was also a star-faring civilization nearby, in the early-development stage of actually navigating their solar system. They were close, allowing the

Movement a chance to not only help but grow with this race of beings, similar to the ancient history of the twin planets of his own system. Together they could start a new order of peace and prosperity, maybe even becoming strong enough to keep the Imperium at bay. Urzzt had seen enough of corruption! To many, it was exciting that they had made the journey to this system. It had barely been surveyed, and even less visited by anyone from the Imperium. Urzzt had aspirations for his people to even teach these carbon-based organisms to travel outside their system. Someday they would even teach them about the worlds they'd come from... but not the darkness also found there. This new world could become the foundation for a whole new expanse based on the foundations of Peace and Coexistence, not tyranny and oppression. Urzzt had such hopes for their fortunes in this new place. Maybe this would be the pinnacle of the Movement.

Maybe meant nothing now. The ship was in chaos as fear had struck its wicked blow against the whole of their people, again. These ... Humans... had just murdered their leaders' peace envoy. *Maybe* now meant that once again they were going to have to fight, in order to create Peace and Harmony. *Maybe* meant Urzzt would have to kill.

***

Urzzt was sickened with grief as he hustled down the dark, musty corridor toward one of the shuttles. Shuttles weren't much use in combat against fleets found just about anywhere in the Imperium, but alas these dozen or so vessels were all they had with any combat capability outside of the Colony ship herself. And there was an armada of treacherous Humans out there, obviously bloodthirsty for violence.

The Imperium had actually designed these as multipurpose vessels; to be used as shuttles, ferries, tugs, and lastly an armed lifeboat. *No,* he thought, *more a distraction to enemies so that the CX-M4 could escape than a lifeboat.* If all else failed, these shuttles would stay behind and harass aggressors so the Colony ship could escape. The Herald was armed, but in its day it would be escorted by a small flotilla of Imperium Military vessels. Especially if hostilities were expected. The shuttles would be used to ferry citizens ship-to-ship or to a surface for survey operations prior to colonization. In fact, Urzzt didn't even know how many such shuttles there were on this ship, nor their true capabilities until the last few dinds. He was a passive being, and never strong enough mentally nor technically to know things like ship statistics, crew requirements, nor things like classes of ships in the Imperium. What he did know was that Shuttle Six was now his command, his chance to do more for his people than just sit and watch others do the hard work to achieve Harmony.

Urzzt had one true love that had preceded the harmony of the Movement. That love was piloting. He had been blessed to explore the Imperium and himself piloting a variety of transport and entertainment vessels before the demise of the Movement. "Too bad," they had told him at his Combat Evaluation Time, that he was "too afraid to put his talent to *real* use as a Peace Keeper in the Imperium. Or even the Magistrate's Special Forces!" After his mandatory couple GCs of time in the Military, piloting cargo haulers and shuttling the *real officers*, he was literally documented as a "Pacifist" by the Combat Evaluation Committee and dumped back into civilian life without opportunity to reenlist. Oh, how he had been thankful for that! He had thought often how little else would make him more soul-sick than being a violent instrument in War. *Have we learned nothing since the last bloody conflict?*

Urzzt straddled Shuttle Six's Pilot/Commander pedestal and waited for the lock-in sequence to secure his four legs for operations. The machinations went about their duty mindlessly, but Urzzt's mind was far from it. He was stricken with a foreboding as he reflexively began his start-up routine, getting the shuttle systems tested and on line. One of his upper arms began toggling engine controls while the other mindlessly entered the sensor and tie-in codes on the other overhead console to update nav, sensor, and tactical data to the vessel. The vessel shuddered as the engine core was brought to life from its lengthy slumber attached to this sixty-plus-GC-old vessel. His lower left arm swept along the ship movement controls back and forth as he re-acquainted himself with the nearly-universal controls of Imperium small craft. With over thirty sentient creature species in the Imperium, it was hard to do, but one of their great technical achievements in the Imperium had been spent two-hundred or so GC ago using vast resources to standardize all controls. The Imperium had made controls *and* ship terminology as universal as possible, even across the three size categories of citizens. A Nurunt from Guutula would be too large to pilot *this* shuttle, but they might be able to squeeze two into the cargo area and connect a control system appropriate for their size! His fourth arm nervously picked at the seams of his chitinous chest-plates, like it was just making sure he was still okay for flight.

It had been almost a thousand GCs in the Imperium since there had been any kind of war, up until this last horrible conflict. And it had been the most bloody of *civil* wars. The whole affair was a derisive commentary on the state of the Imperium; so much so that citizens such as himself had to literally flee what had been hailed as the Epicenter of Peace, in order to find sanctum. It was so sad, that in their own society....

"Pilot, glad you're already here. Get me a sit-rep on systems immediately and I'll then bring you and Gurun – did I say that right? – up to speed on the most recent tactical situation and plans." The sound tore at him, as the voice would always be an abrasive sound to any Drenn or Drenn-uth from his home worlds. It was the sound of a Rayzuud using ISIL, the Imperium Standard Integrated Language, which was used universally within the Imperium. But spoken words from a Rayzuud were still a blend of screeching and gnashing sounds from the toothed beak which was only part of their monstrous appearance. The Rayzuud species, and this particular specimen, hailed from the planet called "Let" which was far from hospitable to Urzzt's race. The Rayzuud were short, feathered serpent/lizards,with wings and four muscular limbs. Compared to other common Imperium species, with only four limbs and a flattened tail, the Rayzuud were quite odd. Rumors still say that the Rayzuud trace their heritage back

221

to a time as airborne predators; but no self-respecting authority will acknowledge that these dense, massive creatures ever would have had the ability to fly on their own. It was a sore spot of pride to the Rayzuud. "I'm glad you're Commander on this, Urzzt" she screeched out, "It's pretty bad if these Humans have any decent space-war capabilities. The Council is in an uproar, and even now debating a full annihilation response. Assuming they haven't totally underestimated these Humans." That last word was exceedingly excruciating on Urzzt as she settled into the chair that would accommodate her physiology at the right station.

Luckily, Vereenda couldn't see the wincing in his mandibles nor the erratic shaking of his unoccupied arm across his chest and leg-plates as his talon had dragged itself across his chest plate. With her surprise entrance he hadn't had the chance to brace for the auditory assault of her voice. It wasn't really that bad when he was ready, especially since he and Vereenda were friends, but Rayzuud speech would always remain a painful sound - like claws across the ceramic hull of an old cargo-runner. The thought alone caused his back spines to shudder. Luckily, Vereenda was distracted as another citizen from his home-planet of Ula entered the shuttle bridge.

"Vereenda! Urzzt! Nice to see you both again, sorry it's under these circumstances."

The equivalent of a stern "Ahem!" came from Vereenda.

"Sorry. Protocols for you military lifer folk. Gurun reporting as left gunner and engineer on shuttle...um, what shuttle is this anyway?"

"Six" said Urzzt, knowing Gurund just said that to irk Vereenda.

"Six? Reporting to Six. I hope that's someone's lucky number on this ship, it's sure not mine. I think mine is nine. Is it too late to request a transfer to nine?" Gurun smiled, for a Drenn-uth, which was never something that translated well. It looked like an aggressive display of the mandibles with some added fang and maw behind. It was about as good as the Drenn and Drenn-uth could do, as their species weren't really good with verbal communication and displays with such minimal complexity. "Permission to come aboard or transfer to Shuttle Nine?"

"Permission granted" replied Urzzt with a slight snicker. He hoped Vereenda hadn't perceived that nor how he hadn't specified his answer.

"Great, I've got the only two Drenn comedians in the Universe today. I just hope you two are still laughing when you hear what I have to say."

She went into her pre-flight briefing, as was the Tactical Officer's privilege. Until the vessel was actually moving under power, standard military protocol held that the assigned Tactical officer had to clear the vessel and personnel for launch. It was a good check, having someone else assess the condition of the Pilot who was also usually Commander of tiny vessels. Vereenda droned on about the situation – but Urzzt was in a different place mentally. He got the basics, that there were thirteen large combat-vessels, a few ships that seemed to be supply or support ships, and an abundant number of tiny craft. There were two groups of ships...etc, and Vereenda went on about the makeup of the enemy fleet. Meanwhile, Urzzt wandered back to thinking about how they'd all fled bloodshed and violence, the near annihilation of the Movement and billions of citizens in the last Civil War, only to come here and experience this. His soul already mourned for the children of the next generation.

***

Fortunately, tactics were simple in a shuttle. Especially when compounded by their dire situation, as dramatically laid out by Vereenda. There was a great flurry of orders and plans between shuttles. There were more of these Human vessels than thought possible at this stage of their development. Apparently, the rumors were quite true that they were both highly adaptive and highly aggressive. The Swarm Tactic, basically concentrating on large targets with their entire force, made sense given the odds against them. Swarm the enemy vessels, starting with those involved in destroying their diplomatic envoy, and then destroy the rest of the enemy fleet. Special focus should be given to any vessels deemed to be a high threat to their CX-M4 home ship.

Since the Colony-Class vessels weren't meant to be combat ships, they weren't set up with the tactical systems of vessels meant for violence. The CX-M4 class was meant for peace, and designed for one main combat tactic: running away. Her defensive weapons were mainly long-range missiles and point defense which also acted as short-range weapons given her size. And the shuttles. She didn't have tactical combat net capabilities, tactical stations for battle control, nor anything really meant to lead any tactical encounters. She could communicate (comm) with only one ship at a time, run away, and settle on a planet. Pretty simple. At best, she may have been slaved to the military combat network during a fight. This meant that while the shuttles had basic orders and tactical doctrine supplied now, they would be on their own after launch. Each vessel would manifest their own destiny.

As they launched, Urzzt regurgitated onto the deck below him as the gravities – literally and figuratively – of the situation struck him hard. It was a small amount on the deck, which he hoped wouldn't be noticed since the other two sat behind and slightly above him. Ironically, his was the most armored position, nestled the furthest forward just behind the main nose weapon – which didn't make him feel all that secure. Urzzt decided he had been wrong about the two-hundred fifty GC old law governing that shuttles and other attached vessels to any colony or exploration-class ship were to be armed. They were still in a sixty-plus-GC-old craft that had never been used, but at least this gave his people a chance, ironically, to defend themselves and the Movement from extermination.

The Herald wasn't defenseless, of course. She had destroyed the ship of Human treachery almost immediately after it had killed the Envoy. But the ship was the most precious piece of hardware they had, and Urzzt knew they shouldn't risk serious harm to her. The loss or severe damage of the Herald would basically mean the end of their way of life, as the ability to create a new habitat would die with the ship. *Maybe no one is getting out of this swamp*, thought Urzzt. He had a duty to perform, a mission to lead, and their way and the right of life to protect. *Can you put pacifism on hold?* he wondered. *Better yet, can I? Can I break the very moral fiber of my belief to protect that belief?*

A Pacifist March to War

It's a moral paradox. I've obviously decided since I'm here, but I wonder what happens once I'm really a part of this. What happens to the divinity of my soul?

Shuttle 6 launched and circled under the belly of the Herald in a slow roll along the hull as it made its way toward the rest of the shuttles and the Human vessels. There were several large enemy vessels, but those smaller ships associated with the murderous villains were decreed to be dealt with first. So they joined with their brethren and descended mercilessly upon the first vessel they came to, similar in size and capabilities to the blistered hulk floating in silent death along the wreckage of their Envoy's Transport Pod. The Swarm was a storm upon their armor and shields - the vessel fell quickly. It was obvious that the destroyed ship had been a different physical design, but similar in function and displacement. Oddly though, it didn't really seem to have any different capabilities. Perhaps that was some sort of camouflage for these beings, to have vessels of different design do the same things? Seems very disordered, but possibly effective against more tactical opponents. This subterfuge may help if they survive as a species into the future. Unfortunately, destruction seems to share common traits across the galaxy, as these vessels die in a similar way to their own. Urzzt hoped everyone had been too busy to notice that he hadn't fired his nose-cannon during the first assault. Instead he had made sure the others had ideal attack angles... or what he thought were ideal.

"I recommend an approach of negative twenty-eight dash seven from ten, twenty-three, eighteen, zero plane... mark, sir" came the comment from Vereenda regarding the next target and approach she had identified. Even though he was never really a true warrior, Urzzt still understood the meaning of approach and attack vectors. Basically, attack vectors in space are three-dimensional and vessels usually use themselves as the first assumed reference point and the target as the destination. Based on her instructions, he moved their shuttle ten degrees up, twenty-three degrees to the right, and eighteen keeds in distance to where he would start an attack run. From there, and using the same plane orientation that he is on now, he would move on a downward angle of twenty-eight degrees toward the target. To make it simple though, he could just follow the navigation screen to the little green light and use the plane gauge to match the shuttle plane to the one Vereenda had entered.

Urzzt hardly had to maneuver to avoid enemy fire. This disturbed him more than actually needing to take evasive maneuvers, as he was allowed to think about the sentient beings whom had just lost their lives. They silently exploded or suffocated or burned in a ball of cleansing fire not for their own actions, but due to the actions of others of their species. This was something they were trying so hard to get away from by coming all this way. And here he was, right in the middle of the abhorrent violence he had sought so hard to avoid. While he convinced himself he had not been directly responsible for the killing of these Humans, he knew had a hand in it. But it didn't feel like the morbid sense of change he'd expected. He was reminded of an old Dreth philosopher's comment on the proliferation of violence – that one hand wrought and soaked in blood only begets more more violence, as all the hands strive toward balance and equality, and the other three seek what they do not have. It never really made sense until he thought of it in today's experience. It made him think about whether the others were having similar dilemmas. He wasn't sure if he was wrong to hope so.

It didn't take long for their superiority to show. These Humans had tenacity and a true talent for violence, if not a real understanding of space nor knowledge of space-war tactics. After all, the Imperium had been conducting war in space for over three thousand GC. While these Humans had hundreds of tiny vessels, which collectively had the power to cause significant destruction if they acted together, they didn't seem to understand how to wield their own power. Several of the tiny vessels working together could hurt or damage a shuttle, but it would take even more to destroy one. And they didn't have the Capital-Class ships to destroy them and the Herald in any prolonged engagement, at least not with these tactics and the firepower they were using. *No*, thought Vereenda, *the only logical explanation was that they held in reserve a secret weapon – something of massive power and brutality would be fitting from these savages.* She had seen in their entertainment vids the way that Humans seemed to become brilliant at the hour of their demise and would always discover some way to defeat their enemies. Standard in entertainment, but they were quite adept and seemed to believe in lulling their opponents into a false sense of victory - but she would see to it that they never had the chance to produce this weapon – or she would die making sure of that this day!

She was familiar with the Human propensity for violence. *They had never known peace during the history that the Imperium knew they were in this system. How could a rag-tag bunch of miscreant religious rejects hope to defeat a battle-hardened species with just a Colony-Class ship and a dozen shuttles? In their own system?* She startled herself with that thought, for she hadn't thought about the advantages of this being their home system. *They could be ready to ambush us as well! It was folly for the Movement leaders to think this would go well, wasn't it? Even if the Humans are defeated here, they must follow some sort of logic and maintain a much stronger fleet protecting the inner defenses of their home world. Just because they couldn't find that fleet from here didn't mean it wasn't out there, waiting in the dark with murderous intent! But she would find a way to circumvent their treachery while overcoming any of their advantages here. She had to!*

"Gurun, enhance sensors for tactical sweep of this fourth planet, plus the asteroid ring within, let's say, twenty degrees of our current battle scene." *Think think think.* "If the Humans were ready here, and planned this aggressive attack, they could have an ambush ready and incoming. With our forces heavily engaged here, the threat of attack from behind would force us to retreat from this system!"

"Aye Tactical Officer. Reconfiguring sensors and direction. This will reduce fine tactical sensors in the combat area on average by Forty-four percent, possibly more if we receive large amounts of debris or other data to classify." Gurun made it clear that he didn't like the idea. "Perhaps The Herald should reconfigure and we'll draw from them instead?" he shot back.

227

"Commander. Preference on sensor information?" She was willing to defer to Urzzt. She knew he would want the first chance at whatever they might discover, before someone decided to get them into even worse violence.

Great, infighting already. Urzzt thought carefully about it. "Go with Vereenda's plan, Gurun. I can handle this bucket out here with just visual sensors at this point. The potential danger to Herald is too great to worry about our own situation. Once we know that the hundred-thirty thousand on her are safe from ambush, we can bring full sensors into this battle. For now, let's put forward sensors on visual at the moment and keep our flanks and tail with the majority. I think we can spot the targets with visual and tactical for now!"

"Aye sir" came the unified response from Vereenda and Gurun.

The Swarm had gone on to destroy another of the Human Destroyer vessels and were maneuvering to join the battle with one of the two largest Human ships, when the lead shuttle, shuttle 1 actually, was torn into by a concentrated salvo from the sizable enemy ship. It wasn't a surprise that it had died under that much fire, but it sent Vereenda's mind racing as she evaluated options based on the unending onslaught of tactical data coming in from not only her sensors, but those of all the shuttles networked into the Swarm link.

"Swinging out into four-pronged claw attack on nose of enemy capital ship!" came Urzzt's confirmation moments after her tactical recommendation appeared on his screen.

"You're a testament to the reflexes of your people. And pilots everywhere, Urzzt." Standard praise from Vereenda, something she'd said often back in the military.

The remaining eleven shuttles splintered into four different directions across the nose of the enemy ship and concentrated fire into the same section from four different angles. That tactic was well known to saturate point-defense with enough attacking ships of their limited armament. In the Imperium though, against a true combat vessel, it would have required at least a dozen more shuttles to overcome the armor of a capital ship of this size. *Luckily these aren't Imperium ships!* They poured pulsed plasma fire into an area in the nose of that large ship, right above the markings "C H I L E" which made for a nice reference point for coordinated targeting lights. The ship's defensive fields folded rapidly and several strikes made it through not only the shielding but armor, noticeably damaging the hull. A large chain of silent explosions burst outward in a dance of light and radiation as fire and Humans were hurtled outward into the darkness of space.

Shuttle 6 jockeyed its way through the sudden debris field and Vereenda noticed again that they had struck with only the two side cannons. She sent a private station-station message to Gurun asking for a damage assessment on all systems. It was safe to assume that Urzzt was still conflicted on the purpose of combat actions to achieve peace. He knew academically, as she had often discussed with him, that most often violence had been used in the Imperium to create or maintain a lasting peace. That, however, was something a pacifist like Urzzt just had trouble wrapping his cranium around. "How do you shun peace in the hopes of achieving peace?" he used to say. To which she often replied, "Peace requires a terrible sacrifice to achieve, and a willingness to further sacrifice ones own purity in order to maintain. Peace is not for the faint of heart nor ill-advised." He understood the meaning, but it was a matter of faith in that violence that he never seemed to get from her. For now, she presumed, she would allow him that without confrontation. She just had to adjust her own tactical plans, again.

Few had the ability to truly master facilitating the Swarm link, but Vereenda excelled at multitasking her station duties with jumping into other ships and evaluating their data and visual readings, as well as the sensor data from all the vessels. She had missed the opportunity to see the death of Shuttle 1, as she was searching for signs of the ambush and working on sensor tuning, but she watched it on the images stored in Shuttle 9 which had been recording the live data from Shuttle 1. She shared her evaluation and assessment with the other networked Tactical Officers and found herself in heated debates regarding the need for the Humans to concentrate their weak fire into volumes that could overwhelm shuttle defenses. It didn't appear that the Colony Vessel would be in an significant danger in this battle, assuming they could keep the majority of Human combat vessels at bay. So the leaders had chosen to keep the Herald here and could engage as necessary. She knew that it was ego and the pent-up frustration at the Imperium that was driving them now. They seemed different than before this journey, like they had reached the end of their patience. Their pride and arrogance were already taking over, evident as they had already begun to debate about how to deal with the Human home-world, called Earth, once the battle was finished and Colonization had begun.

"Vereenda!" came an outburst from Gurun. "I've got what appears to be a small group of tiny enemy vessels inbound fast from the region toward the asteroid belt. They're meeting with another group of tiny vessels on the other side of the Herald!"

Damn! "Pilot, break off this run and bring us around after that grouping." She wasn't quite shouting, but the urgency was clear, and should be to any species. Vereenda shot her sensor information out as urgent to the other shuttles, as another Human ship was being torn apart by the other ten. She updated her tactical data as the shuttle she had thought destroyed before was making attacks of opportunity at tiny craft as they swept by to follow them. If they were able to restore their drive system, that would be phenomenal!

"Headed there now. Overtake them near the end of their run along the length of the Herald. We have five other shuttles along-side and in the same basic pursuit course. We'll have them down the left side from current plane. I'll roll us ninety degrees, giving both you and Gurun angles of attack on the squadron." Urzzt responded. He tried to sound confident and robotic, as if he were emotionless.

Vereenda couldn't really take Urzzt's scheme any longer – did he really plan to fight in this war without doing any of the dirty work himself? "We'll have a better tactical advantage if we yaw inward on the enemy vessels, allowing us to get all weapons to bear on them. I'd estimate a ten percent tactical increase per vessel with that. Preference, Commander?" She skewed the last word, perhaps not as subtly as she'd wished.

"I'd rather keep main thrust in a vector that leads us in our optimal path and speed, allowing for the most escape routes and options after the attack. With this route, I think we'll have a good chance at returning to engage further enemy craft." Urzzt was lying. *Obviously to her*, he thought. He just wasn't ready. He could yaw toward the fighters and still have a variety of options, which Vereenda and Gurun probably knew, but he wasn't ready and he didn't need everyone outside knowing it too.

"Understood Commander." Vereenda decided not to push it. *Besides,* she thought, I *have my own conflict to deal with. I don't need to keep pushing his. Or do I?*

"I'll be ready, sir!" came the response from Gurun as he stressed the "sir!" with a smile. He found this all quite intriguing, actually. "The humans call them "fighters" if that helps with tactical designation, Vereenda. Interesting for such obviously small and ineffective vessels, don't you think, Urzzt? "Fighters," yet not really so much of a fight."

No reply came, though, as Urzzt was busy in his own mind wondering about when he was going to have to actually kill one of those "fighter" vessels. It didn't seem like his abstinence would last this day.

The six shuttles descended upon the Human fighters, which had split into two sets. They were obviously moving to flanking positions, from which to better attack regardless of which group the shuttles engaged. It was a futile gesture, in Urzzt's mind, as they seemed oblivious or blind to the five shuttles swinging around what would be *their* flank. As well, they now split their fire concentration, which was already a problem for getting through the measly shuttle defenses. The fighters didn't seem to understand how quickly those shuttles could be upon them, nor the extent of their own frailty. These aliens were so, well, "alien." As Urzzt twisted Shuttle 6 into its roll, with the top presented to the enemy fighter group that had been chosen, both Vereenda and Gurun began firing on vessels within their firing arcs. Shuttle 3 moved through their ranks quickly into the most prominent enemy focal position, yawing into the position so that the nose was pointed directly at the one enemy group as they slid sideways, allowing them to fire all three weapons at the enemy fighters. Shuttle 3 was rewarded for her aggressiveness with a concentrated attack by all the enemy fighters on that well-presented nose, which overwhelmed its point defense and allowed enemy fire to damage the forward section. As its nose section had been riddled with holes, Urzzt and Gurun felt at least one life blink out of existence around them. As a telepathic species, Drenn were quite attuned to the presence of life around them, but even more so to other members of their species. There obviously was or had been a Drenn or Drenn-uth on that Shuttle.

Urzzt felt something else quite odd as they slid past the enemy fighters. Perhaps because he wasn't busy shooting at the aliens, he was able to feel the presence of two beings in their fleet, not the dozen or so that lifeforms he would expect, assuming even just one Human per vessel. And then Gurun picked up on it from Urzzt. They began a back and forth telepathic discussion, knowing it would take far too long audibly. If they were right, and they both did agree, then this would mean that they were killing far less Humans than Urzzt had feared! Urzzt was suddenly disturbed that he found joy and hope in being part of killing *less* beings of the Universe.

"Tactical update, Vereenda." Urzzt couldn't hide his enthusiasm for this information.

"I'm not finding any new information, Commander." she replied. "What have you got?"

"Oh, this is going to be lovely" chortled Gurun.

"Shell it, Gurun." shot Urzzt. "Enemy fighter group contains two..." He suddenly felt one of the lives blink out of existence "correction, one, Human life sign. It appears that the majority of Human fighters are actually automatons or at least don't seem to be carrying Humans. Presence Sense shows only one remaining Human. I recommend we cease random destruction and wipe out automated vessels only. There are also..."

"Wait wait wait! Presence Sense? Out here and at this distance? I don't understand, Urzzt. These aren't Drenn or Drenn-Uth. How can you tell anything from them, let alone in combat conditions. And why isn't anyone else noticing." She knew all the Drenn and Drenn-Uth were telepathic with that creepy Presence Sense, but during combat operations and sensing a species they'd never encountered? *Urzzt must be letting his personal conflict over killing get to him. I guess he really is a pacifist, with no stomach for killing at all.*

"Actually Tactical, I am noticing it too" added Gurun. "Well, not right now since they are pursuing the five shuttles who did the most damage as they struck by. However, when we were close, I could also at least tell they were there. Not to the extent Urzzt did, but that may be because he is less...distracted... than I am."

"Fine, fine!" She shot back. *How the hell do I explain this over the Swarm link?* "If that's the case, I think we all know that if you're going to kill a Bordubi Raantakg, you don't just rip off eight of its pincer arms and wait - You have to take the head! Wouldn't it make sense, Commander, to kill the Human pilot assuming they're the head of the beast?"

"Yes, perhaps it would. But in this case my orders, on this ship, will be that we DO NOT destroy targets identified with living pilots. If we are to ever coexist with these creatures, it will be good to have shown them mercy at the beginning. Is that understood?!" He wasn't quite shouting, but he found himself shaking as bio-energy surged through his system, responding to the strain of emotions he didn't even want to think about. He took Vereenda's silence as understanding. *This isn't a military ship and we're not a bunch of killers!* he followed up but only to himself. *Vereenda's drive for glory seems to have a headcount attached to it. Well, she'll just have to gain honor and glory without killing. Maybe she'll get extra karma for winning the hard way!*

***

Their trap, as it had been called, had not gone quite as foreseen. This particularly alien pilot, a peculiar and quite lethal Human adversary already tagged as a "High Threat" by the Council, had actually proceeded exactly as they had foreseen. At the last possible moment, nearing the precise location they wanted him, he flipped his tiny ship and accelerated away from the kill zone. Away from the cover and protection of the incoming fighters and the Human fighter-transport vessel. It had been a gamble to try and herd them into a single location, but it seemed like this Human had been toying with *them*, not the other way around! It made Urzzt sigh quietly in relief, though, as he had no interest in killing en masse. *I just need more time to discover the way to peacefully end this! There must be Humans who want peace as much as I do. I can't accept that the Universe is full of such blood lust that all Humans are the monsters Vereenda sees out there!*

Seven of the shuttles were now pursuing high-threat Human fighter, with two re-tasked and headed toward the fighter transport. As the seven rolled into kill positions behind the enemy, he started to navigate a debris field thus dodging several plasma blasts. The lead shuttle fell under attack suddenly as several explosions burst across its hull.

"It's the debris! It identified as harmless in the system because it wasn't powering weapons!" shouted Vereenda as several more sprang to life, firing beam weapons and exploding if they came into close proximity with a shuttle. "They're mines! The Humans are using mines!" She had added that last to the Swarm tactical comms as that lead shuttle, Shuttle Four, sputtered and began listing in a dead roll.

"Mines have been outlawed for four hundred GC!" shot Gurun, disgustedly. "These shuttles are not equipped with tactical sensors and wouldn't know a mine field if they saw one!" He was clearly defensive about the shuttle's inability to detect them. "These Humans are horrific! Perhaps Quizl was right to have thought we should wipe them all out before they irrevocably harm the rest of us!"

"I'm pushing through behind the shuttle in front of us!" Urzzt knew that this would not sit well with the Council. Even now there was debate regarding the future of Humanity. "Presuming they're even right that we'll survive this encounter!"

"Who is right, Urzzt?" Vereenda shot back, laughing nervously.

"Someday I'll stop talking to *myself* around you, Vereenda. Who knows what kind of trouble I may get into!" Urzzt remembered the last time he had been talking to himself while with Vereenda. They had almost been discovered by one of the Council minions! He smiled at the thought of them hiding in the ventilation again, someday.

She didn't reply, though. She was frantically trying to tag all the mines their antiquated shuttle sensors could detect. She knew they would have to come back for them else these mines drift through the system and harm friend or foe alike, directly or indirectly, in the future. Imperium law dictated that ancient mines, if discovered, were required to be tagged and reported or recovered. As the forward surge pulled her back on her grav chair, she could see enemy fighters converging on the remains of shuttle Four while shuttle Eight began a turn to defend them. "I've got no life-signs on Four, Eight! Don't sacrifice yourselves to those monsters for an empty shuttle! Let the Humans swarm our dead while we take their living!" She could feel her scales lifting and feathers flattening with anger! It was her turn to talk to herself, "We came in peace, and this is the way savages receive us..." she continued her tirade, soothing her rage as she fought waves of impulses to tear apart the interior of their shuttle.

Gurun could see Vereenda changing demeanor, starting to fall apart mentally as well, as she continued her rant about the primitive Humans and their disease of violence. *I guess Vereenda's pro-extermination.* As Vereenda leaned back and peered at the ceiling, a Rayzuud method of calming down by aligning their frame or something, he wondered if the individuals in the Imperium had felt that way about the Movement. *Did we not see how our internal conflicts within the Movement had spilled out on the false veil of peace and civility in the Imperium?* He took in a deep, long, cleansing breath. *Whether it was false or not, the citizens had been content with the Imperium. The factions of the Movement had soured everyone with their pettiness and violence. Violence done for peace is often necessary, but undesirable. The violence done by the Movement hadn't been necessary.* Gurun was motionless at the revelation. *So the Imperium only saw violence in them, not reasons nor the pain it caused many of the followers. Oh no, we WERE becoming a scourge on society!*

"Gurun! Gurun!" Urzzt was practically shouting as he finally turned to see Gurun's distant visage returning to the present. "Put the shield emitters in your section up to priority. I don't need speed as much as we need you to keep this bucket flying! I don't want to explain to your mate that you didn't make it back because you were daydreaming instead of keeping your damned shield emitters working!" He said the last with a joking tone hoping whatever was going through his head would clear up.

Gurun entered the change for the automated repair systems and then moved around to the opposite side, pulling apart the cover panels to repair his damaged station. He was glad to be the only one who should ever get up and move about during combat. *If I weren't the Engineer I'd be stuck in that damned seat!*

Urzzt turned back toward his visual scanners and ran his third hand's claws along the visual outline of the enemy fighter. *It was like a drop of rain in the night,* he thought, *with a fleeting beauty all its own. And yet a devastating nightmare when traveling at great speeds massed with its companions. Perhaps that was the inspiration for the*

Humans' tiny craft? They are like the torrential rains or the great tidal waves of Floreteen Prime. If the Humans had ever seen that world, they would understand the comparison. He continued to study the fighter, then magnified a section off the fighter's nose. There were two distorted reflections there.

"Vereenda, what are those?" Urzzt had sent the feed to Vereenda's tactical screen. As she slowly dropped her head, serenity filling her soul again, she lurched upright in a guttural yell, which the Universe never heard.

***

"Gurun, what's our status?" Urzzt opened his eyes in pairs, checking his spectrum of vision as he realized he was looking through the faceplate of his emergency helmet into the darkness, as only the occasional spark lit the interior of the shuttle. "Vereenda?! Gurun?!" A shower of electrical sparks lit up the sections behind his station as he turned toward Vereenda's tactical station. He could already see her form slumped over sideways in the seat. He started tearing at his pedestal, pulling the manual release for his legs so that he could get to her station.

Vereenda was being illuminated, even after the fountain of sparks had ceased, in a pure starlight reflected off the interior consoles through the tear in the hull near her station. As he crossed the light's path, the shadow he cast softened the blow as he observed the upper right side of her body pancaked into the backing of her station from a significant impact. Her helmet and mask were on but crushed along that side, with a cruel fracturing across the entire helmet. It must have been torture for her as her chest heaved, sputtering sounds and liquid-filled breath resounding behind the helmet. *What have I done?* She lurched in a pain he couldn't comprehend and he could hear more fluid hit the inside of her faceplate through her comm device. He dropped to the floor in front of her and grabbed the med kit out of the bin below her feet. As he stood, placing it on her lap for access, she used her torn left arm to push the lid closed. He couldn't see her face, or what was left of it, but he only imagined the grimace as she gurgled something quiet and faint into the comm microphone. He looked past the destruction and chaos inside the bridge, toward the weapons cabinet. It was twisted and inaccessible where the left wing had been practically sheared away. He knew how strong she was, even for a Rayzuud, that she was alive even now. He stared at her for a few long moments, contemplating if he could do what she wanted. Thinking about how they would no longer "rendezvous," as they called it, to talk or just be with each other.

He pulled a long breath and took off his mask, knowing that he could survive long enough in the vacuum to do this one thing for her. He pulled himself gently over her body, straddling the chair and her bracing his four legs for support, then put his bare face to her helmet while slowly lowering the hidden fangs. He could feel her nudge her face to his, silently returning his affection and gesturing her approval. With what must have been great pain, she wrapped her left arm around him in a stern hug as he caressed the back of her shoulder. And then he sank the venomous fangs right through her suit, into the shoulder. As a man of peace, he had despised those accursed fangs most of his life. Now he nearly cried that they were available to him. She didn't shudder nor jump at the bite, she just held him even stronger until the venom did its work. Urzzt had known that he would have to kill. But this made his soul feel worse than he could imagine. "I'm sorry I failed you so completely," he said as he gently slid away from her and crumbled to the floor at her feet. He put on his helmet and tasted the now-bitter gift of life it generated. He just sat quietly, praying for both their souls now.

Urzzt had no idea how long he'd sat on the floor, but he had work to do and at least one more life to maintain. He turned toward the light source shining down upon Vereenda's body, and found he was looking through a large tear from practically the nose to mid ship, with this system's yellow star and probably tons of cosmic rays flowing into the interior. He turned toward the Engineer station to see if Gurun had managed to survive, but found only a helmet floating there with a spattering of green fluid, similar to their species' internal fluids. There was another tear in the hull over there as well. Urzzt called out and searched for Gurun, to no avail. He could see the tattered wing outside the left side of the shuttle, practically falling away as he peered through the darkness into the shadows beneath it. As he started to search for tools and catalog damage, power flickered on but only briefly. After the initial startle, he was overjoyed at the likelihood that the power source was still functional. With Gurun gone and Vereenda dead, Urzzt knew he was unlikely to fix the ship before the Humans had destroyed him, but he had to focus on something. He didn't care for the shuttle being his new floating tomb, and the prospect that he had a chance was enough for him. He couldn't stay exposed to space for long, though, and the cosmic rays of the star could soon overwhelm him. Assuming something like space-debris didn't kill him first.

First things first, he thought, as he cleared a workspace amongst the littered chaos of the interior. He set out the repair tools which had thankfully been found secured in their compartments. He grabbed the emergency sealant and crawled out onto the exterior of the hull, waiting only for the helmet to adjust to the brightness out here. He had never tried repairing a ship this damaged nor from the *outside* like this, but there was a serenity out here as the Universe seemed to whisper softly to him. The broken shuttle was floating along, without violent spins nor tumbling. He wondered if he should just sit down out here and watch the lights of the battle or the wonders of the cosmos until he succumbed to it.

The ship was torn from nose to stern on both sides, right above where Vereenda and Gurun's stations sat. *The damage doesn't look so bad from out here*, he thought, standing atop the symbol for six. He sprayed the hull sealant into the gash, layering it upon itself in order to cross the expanse and seal the tear. He stopped for a moment to look at Vereenda's peaceful body through the opening before he sealed it. *Was it the right thing for her? It felt right at the time, but I wonder if she could have been saved?* He turned away as he contemplated that question and finished sealing the gash. He quickly moved down toward the nose of the ship, sealing across the opening all the way.

Then Urzzt moved to the other side, in order to seal across and over Gurun's empty station. Maybe 2-3 kips away from him, just out of reach, he found Gurun's body floating in an end-over-end slow spin. It was grossly distorted from direct damage, twisted in a look of terror or anguish, with the obvious effects of explosive decompression. *No one gets left behind, my friend!* He reached a long arm out toward the body, but couldn't reach as it just floated less than an arms length away from his clawed fingers. Urzzt's legs wobbled under the strain, compounded by the venom loss as his body worked to manufacture a new supply. *It would help if I could eat,* he thought as he smelled the burned plating and internal tissue. *Bad sign - My mind's playing tricks on me!* He could taste the sour flavor of the internal fluids, even though the body was frozen here and you couldn't get the smell nor taste in space. *It must be the solar rays. Damn!* Urzzt looked around helplessly, angry at the Universe for slapping him in the face with the body of his friend but not the time to retrieve it right away. In searching for answers amongst the stars he found a pair of alien fighters, beautiful and floating calmly in view out past the body. He stiffened momentarily, fear gripping him until a few more moments had passed and they did nothing. He was suddenly aware of the two lifeforms, and could tell that one was the familiar high-threat pilot they had been pursuing. *Are they wondering what to do with me?* was all he could offer in thought about them. He didn't have time to stay out here any longer. He tried one last futile time to grab hold of Gurun, then dropped his head in self-disgust as he went about sealing the hull. He wondered whether he should return with the mangled body of his friend or leave it to spare his family the sight of it like this. Urzzt wished the Council could be here to see the shredded bodies and destruction within. Maybe they would think more about the importance of life. *But who am I to lecture them? Having taken one of those lives I want them so vehemently to mourn. Maybe violence amongst the sentient lifeforms can't be vanquished after all? I can't accept that. Maybe,* he thought, *won't mean anything unless I can get back to the Council and persuade them to be of peace, not violence.* He watched the Humans for a few more moments, feeling their stares in return, like they had just reached a decision together. It may be a delusion, but he hoped they'd give him the chance to try to change things for the better with his people. Urzzt went back to work filling the tear and other holes, eventually sealing himself into the tomb once again.

***

Urzzt reveled in what he had accomplished. In a short period of time he had been able to get the shuttle into a functional ship! He had been extremely fortunate that main power was still active and had only blown fail-safe connectors due to feedback damage at the tears. He had gotten the diagnostics running with their independent backup power, but nearly drained that power using the training help to restore main power to critical systems. While waiting for the systems to go through their own start-up diagnostics, he watched the sensor and visual playback which captured the two alien fighters bursting from the other fighter's shadow on an intentional intercept course. Had they not altered their courses slightly to avoid the other fighter, he wouldn't be alive to watch the playback. As it were, the alien fighters practically disintegrated after contact with the shuttle's defensive fields and then the physical impacts on the hull. *They killed only two of our three,*, he sneered, *not the one who probably deserved it most.* He didn't know if Humans had piloted those ships, but the tactic was an affront to his being, if so. *These Humans act as if life has little meaning to them. So how do I begin to believe they are not quite so heinous as this act implies? If they truly value life so little, how do I approach that but still give them dignity and respect? In order to open a lasting dialogue for peace.* It was a demoralizing thought. *Not that they deserve our respect.* He finished his solo Rayzuud ceremony, best as he could recall, marking his chest-plate to indicate a Rayzuud warrior's first kill. Right next to the ISIL symbol meaning "Peace" he had etched there before the ceremony. Forever would the mark of peace and the Rayzuud symbol remind him of the bitter reality of such violence, but more importantly it was an honor to the fallen warrior, Vereenda. It was the least he could do for her.

After recovering Gurun's body and repairing a new hole in the hull from a debris strike, Urzzt limped the shuttle back toward the CX-M4 mother ship, checking and cross-checking the systems for any signs of damage or structural failures. Several systems, such as sensors or the comm equipment, were just way beyond his meager technical skill even with the tutelage of the diagnostic program. With only visual sensors functional, he had struggled to even find the massive ship and then orient the shuttle. Luckily, several small and one particularly large explosions had allowed him to zero in on the Colony-Class vessel. As he slowly crept home in the darkness, the self-repair systems got point-defense and shields operational which consequentially allowed weapons systems to come back as a byproduct! "I guess it's good that I'm more worried about debris than chasing the enemy!" He finally took the time to wrap and seal the two bodies as best he could. Locked into his pedestal once again, he yearned only to be able to rest. But he couldn't repair the automated flight systems and he was just too paranoid regarding all the dangers flying around. As he brought the shuttle along a parabolic approach from behind the Herald, he spotted a reflection and light ahead of him.

As Urzzt slowly started to overtake the Colony ship, he had stumbled upon a Human fighter. It appeared to have been surgically dismantled, most likely by one of the asteroid-cutting beams of the Colony ship, indicating it had gotten very very close. Floating among the few sections outside the vessel, much like Gurun's body had been, was an unmoving Human. It was small, with only four limbs, a round head, and no distinguishable facial features. *It's alive!* Urzzt marveled at his ability to sense Humans this easily. *Maybe they're telepathic too? I wonder if Humans require suits for activity in space?* Without sensors he really couldn't tell, except by watching. As he got closer he recognized the presence of the high-threat enemy pilot. After searching for attacking ships, he realized that he was watching it. Had this Human laid the barbaric mines but also decided not to kill him earlier? *Or was his companion the merciful one?*

Urzzt stopped the shuttle relatively close to the Human, watching from the darkness. Eventually the Human woke up and proceeded to go about repairing his vessel, much as Urzzt had not that long ago. As he followed the Human's actions, much like a predator stalking its prey, he was often distracted by the signs of battle far ahead as the Herald stayed in view but was moving away from him. Sometimes it was obvious that vessels were exploding rather than ordnance.

The Human spent time diligently working to repair the fighter, primarily on the sections lit by the star. Unlike Urzzt's shuttle, the fighter tumbled along, rotating at a difficult-to-manage speed which left the Human moving back and forth quite a bit. Urzzt stayed with the Human, always watching over its shoulder from a distance.

Once the human started struggling on the shadowed side of the ship for repairs, Urzzt decided that now was the time to take the first step toward understanding the Humans. *If it attacks me now, then I'll know they're barbarous in nature. If not, well I don't know yet. Let's just start with a greeting.* He activated the shuttle's lighting array, pouring clear light from the nose of his ship at the Human pilot's back, illuminating the section it was working on. The Human went stiff immediately and Urzzt doubted he would ever be able to explain to a Human the irony of their similar reactions, his being not too long ago. The Human spun around. *Now we'll see what it does!* It waved at him with one of the upper appendages. He didn't know if it meant the same for Humans, but that was a standard greeting in the Imperium. He was stunned and wondered what he should do with this Human. *Maybe it knew something of the Imperium? It was a truly non-aggressive act, implying some semblance of civility. Maybe Human leaders are just as terribly violent and foolhardy as ours?* He watched it roll to the other side, pausing this time before following. His action should be elementary. He felt ashamed when he realized that, until that point, he hadn't really wanted or expected such a civil response. He felt even guiltier for being a part of all the violence, but that guilt made him angry at what the Humans had started out here when they killed the Peace Envoy.

As he swung around to the same side as the Human again, he knew he was at a key point in the destiny of two civilizations. That didn't make him feel any better. He wanted to be the better being and take the harder path, but the anger in him already had his second arm powering up weapons for the easier choice. He knew this pilot had spared him, but he'd been forced to kill Vereenda because of these Humans. *Who am I to decide our fates? Do they deserve Peace? Do we? Maybe none of us deserve to live. Is it my arrogance that even allows me to think that I have the power to sway two civilizations one way or another? Is violence now necessary, but undesirable? Can I be the warrior I've just claimed for Vereenda and the pacifist, both?*

Urzzt screamed as Shuttle Six surged forward, weapons still active, while he continued to struggled with the decision of what to do; knowing only that he could shape the destiny of both Humans and the Movement alike in this moment.

Catalino Tolejano, II *is a Martial Art hacking, Cartoon-watching, Computer nerd-ing, Comic-Con-ing, Triathlon-scrambling, Wedding officiating, Sci-fi geek-ing, RPG-ing, Lawn mowing, M&M collecting, Video gaming, House fixing, Stargazing, Weapon flailing, Self-inflicting, Toy collecting, Uber-dork extraordinaire! All rolled into a Miami Dolphins fan trapped in Wisconsin.*

If you read writing blogs, watch podcasts, attend workshops, and talk to authors – it becomes pretty clear that writing is far more often a skill learned through study, hard work, and practice, rather than simply a natural-born talent possessed by all authors.

AuthorsRising.com *is a place for up-and-coming authors to come together and collaborate on stories, learn from each other, and hone their skills. Authors Rising, LLC publishes collections of those stories, on behalf of the authors involved.*

If you'd like to be a part of one of our books, and are willing to work hard, meet deadlines, and take & give honest, well-intentioned feedback from your fellow authors, come check us out.

We'd love to have you be a part of the community.

www.ingramcontent.com/pod-product-compliance
Lightning Source LLC
Chambersburg PA
CBHW031941240626
47153CB00003B/820